The Light of Deception

The Saints of Savannah Series

Leigh Ebberwein

Old Fort Press
Savannah, Georgia

This book is dedicated in memory of my dad,
Harold Benjamin Horton

1937 - 2025

Your love for Savannah's history inspires me and
will continue to live on through these pages.

Contents

Chapter 1

Find Your Light

Savannah, Georgia

The protective iron gate of Gordonston's park moaned in protest as I pushed my way through. Instinctively, I began searching for my grandfather before remembering he was no longer here. He had passed away the week before. I moved slowly down the path, maneuvering through the many mounds of cracked cement resulting from the live oaks stretching their roots—another reminder that the land in the deep South was here long before its inhabitants.

As I drew closer, I noticed a concrete marker placed in the spot my grandfather always sat. Kneeling down closer, I was able to read it more clearly. "Find Your Light" was chiseled across the stone. I swallowed hard, trying to keep my emotions intact, but felt the cry rise in the back of my throat as the floodgates opened. I placed my hand on the stone, warm from the sun. My heart still ached for a time in the past. I hadn't understood the phrase the first time, so he had been forced to clarify. "There has always been light and darkness. Good and evil.

Happiness and sadness. But hear me, Janine, an artist needs both. It is in darkness that we find our true purpose and in light that we create. You must embrace that darkness before you can find your light!"

I always believed he was referring to his light as his creations, until one early morning when I found him behind his easel, hidden in the back corner of this neighborhood park. I had moved toward him slowly and quietly, not to disturb him, and was surprised to find him quietly crying while his brush gently shaded a portion of his painting. He looked up when he noticed movement but didn't say a word.

"Grandfather, are you all right?" I asked softly.

A faint grin was followed by a small sigh. "I finally found my light," he answered. "I've searched for it for years, and it was right here. Right under my nose. Tucked in the back corner of this garden. I can finally paint again."

Motioning to the canvas, I asked, "May I?" When he nodded, I moved closer. "Wow!" escaped from my mouth in a puff of breath. I couldn't pull my eyes away as I took in every inch of the canvas. I'm not sure if I stood there for one minute or one hundred, but when I finally met his eyes, I was crying, too.

"That's my Paris. My boyhood. From the hills of Mont-martre. The light is exactly the same in this spot. I can see it just as vividly as if I were still there," he answered.

Finally, I mustered up the nerve to ask, "Can you tell me about it?"

"No. Not today," was all he said as he turned back to his painting. Once again, he had been transported to another time and place. I didn't know much about Grandfather Gerard, other than that he had immigrated to Savannah to help a family member who was working on the renovations to the cathedral. It was here that he met my grandmother, an Irish lass whose hair was as fiery as her personality. He was a quiet man who never spoke much about France.

Unfortunately, the day for explanations never came. I never had the opportunity to hear about his childhood in the hilly Paris neighborhood.

I had left the week after my high school graduation, wanting to get as far away from my sleepy little town of Savannah as I could. New York had been my escape. My older sister had moved away ahead of me, buying a bus ticket for as far as she could go with the money in her pocket. Maybe running away was a family tradition, beginning with my grandfather, who had run away from his home in France. I still wonder what he was running from. Possibly, like me, he needed to find a place where no one knew him. A place where he could be himself.

I stood near the edge of the marker he had left there for me. He knew, as an artist, I'd come back to that spot. The beautiful painting he created that day was now hanging above my parents' fireplace. My grandfather had found his light that day, but unfortunately, I was still in search of mine. I'd seen my share of darkness while sketching in New York, but I had never experienced that feeling of light and I desperately wanted to. Right then and there, I decided to move back home and apply for art school.

Chapter 2

Back Home

While I was living in New York, my parents had moved from my childhood home in the Windsor Forest neighborhood and into my grandfather's house, so that they could help care for him as he aged. I'd been home a few times over the years, but I'd always been in a rush. This time, I had nowhere to be.

When I received the phone call about my grandfather's passing, I began packing my bags. Before I fully understood what I was doing, I had packed most of my items in the apartment. "I guess it's time for me to go home," I had told my sister when she got home from work that evening. She hadn't seemed surprised. My granddad's passing was the final tug at my heart, leading me back to Savannah.

I had arrived two nights before, but my sister wouldn't come until the morning of the funeral. Unlike me, her heart still belonged in New York. After pulling my overnight bag from my beat-up Corolla, I slept in the guest room where I had slept several times before at my grandfather's house.

The following morning, as I wandered around the house, I

noticed the mixture of my mom's things and his, intertwined as if they had always belonged together. Old school pictures of my mom, my sister, and me sat side by side on the bookshelf where his classic literature books and my mom's cookbooks leaned on each other, sharing secrets.

"The house looks great, Mom," I told her, hopping on a barstool when I found her in the kitchen.

Her smile warmed my heart as only a mother's smile can do. She left something sizzling on the stove to walk over and kiss my forehead. "It sure is nice to have you home, Jan. I can't tell you how much I've missed you," she said.

I nodded as the scent of bacon and onions filled my senses. "I'm really sorry about Grandfather Gerard. How are you holding up?"

She paused for a brief second before answering. "He's been sick for a long time, but it's never easy losing a parent, even if they are almost ninety." Something popped from the pan and she ran back over to investigate.

"Whatcha cooking this morning?"

"I'm trying to perfect a little dish we had in the Netherlands and put my own twist on it. The Dutch really know how to combine their flavors well. I'm working on my twentieth anniversary cookbook. Can you believe that?"

My thoughts jumped back to a conversation I had with my grandfather years ago in this very kitchen. I had complained about my mom always cooking and wanting to be rich and famous. He had corrected me. "It's not about money or fame. Your mother creates because it brings her joy. Not all artist use charcoal and paint. Surely you see that, being an artist yourself." I hadn't at the time, but I definitely did now.

I answered my mom, "Twenty years creating dishes for the world to enjoy. And your travel photography and images of your prepared meals are beautiful. I'm so proud of you, Mom. And so was Grandfather."

She turned to me as tears began to well in her eyes. "That means the world to me, Jan. Thank you," she whispered before my dad entered the room.

"What are you ladies yammering on about? We've got to get Jan's things moved in. We just need to decide where they're going. You can move into the house, or you can move into the garage apartment. Why don't we go take a look?" he asked.

The garage had been my grandfather's studio and was always off-limits. The place probably smelled like mold and rot. Still, my parents wanted to show it to me. As they led me up the stairs, I realized the boards and handrails were all new, as were a set of wide-paned windows and a freshly painted door with a shiny, brass knocker. But nothing prepared me for the studio apartment with an open floor plan, stylish furniture that looked like it had been ordered straight from the Pottery Barn catalogue, and a bright kitchen with new appliances.

"What's going on here? Did you guys just remodel?"

They sheepishly looked at one another before my mom answered. "Last year, we realized Savannah had become a hot spot for travelers, so we remodeled the studio apartment and have been renting it out as a vacation home."

I let my eyes wander. This place was so nice, much prettier and larger, than any place I had lived in New York. Then reality hit. They had been renting it out. "I can't move in here after all the work you put into this place. Plus, you've been renting it out. I'll just move into one of the bedrooms in the house."

My parents glanced at each other once again. This time, my dad spoke. "You are more important than any renter, and we are so proud of you for deciding to go to art school. We are proud of both of our girls. Y'all haven't asked us for anything since you left Savannah. Do you have any idea how rare that is?"

"Yes, but you wanted us to go off to college, and when we didn't, we knew we must be able to stand on our own two feet. But we sure appreciated all the money you sent us for no good reason."

"We knew you needed to find your own way before coming back to Savannah. We're just thrilled you're back. Now, you can stay in one of the bedrooms in the house, or you can stay in this apartment and pay a small amount of rent. We know you've been working for years in New York and probably have lots of money saved up. The best news is that both of them come with free meals and wi-fi. Either way, we are happy to have you home."

I kissed my mom on the cheek and began to wander around the space. *They think I've saved a lot of money? If only that were true.* I'd barely kept my head above water for the seven years I'd been gone. What did I have to show for it? Nothing. I needed to make some big changes in my life. I continued to walk towards the bedroom area, opening cabinets and closet doors on my way. When I came to a locked door, I asked my parents what was inside.

"Oh yeah," my mom replied. "Locked doors are called 'owner's closets,' but this one is just full of my dad's things that I couldn't give away." She punched in a code and flung open the double doors to a deep closet holding all of my grandfather's art supplies and paintings.

"I'll rent the apartment," I heard myself say as I entered the closet of my dreams. I didn't know how I'd do it, but I had to find a way to make the money to pay for it.

Chapter 3

Suzie's Cake

Over the years, my friends had each come to know my grandfather. So, I wasn't surprised when they all came to his funeral. Although now that I watched them surveying the dishes coming through the door of our after-funeral gathering, I believe I knew the real reason they came—funeral food.

Southerners do things differently from other people; We eat through our emotions. When someone has a baby, breaks their leg, or has a death in the family, we're taking them food. But funeral food is always the best. That's because at funerals you get a smorgasbord of everyone's dishes. Each friend or relative always brings their best dish. Now, it must be delicious, because everyone at the event knows who sent it. In fact, over time, the recipients come to expect certain dishes.

My mom's friend Suzie always sends her iced pound cake. It will sit on the counter, taunting us all, until the appropriate time. There's always order to the gathering, an unsaid set of rules that begin with everyone being called together, followed by the holiest person in the room offering grace, then everyone waits for the "foil lifters" to do their job. They are the people responsible for taking the tin foil off the dishes. As soon as the last glint of silver is removed, everyone will make a beeline to the cake, where they can put a piece on their plate for after their meal. Everyone knows it will run out fast.

I watched my friends scanning the spread of fine Southern cuisine during the prayer, which lasted almost as long as the eulogy itself. Then they made their move. I snickered at the look on their faces when they realized the cake had been removed and began to whisper to one another.

I snuck up behind them. "I think Suzie brought those brownies over there instead of her cake today. And look at Miss Marion's peach cobbler and Mrs. William's banana pudding; they are to die for," I explained.

They turned to me, embarrassed to have been caught. "Oh, honey, this looks amazing," Kathleen answered. She snaked her arm through mine and smiled. "Let's go get in line."

I'd been away for a long time, but I had managed to come back often enough to know they were putting on a show. Still, I followed along.

We each filled our plates with fried chicken, shrimp casserole, BBQ sliders, red rice, mac-and-cheese, and twice-baked potatoes before grabbing a sweet tea and making our way to the back porch.

"Make sure to leave room for dessert," I said as we all settled in at the round table. Everyone grunted quietly in reply. I pretended not to notice.

We had all met our freshman year of high school. And not just any high school, the all-girl Catholic high school in downtown Savannah. We had been the last six girls in the cafeteria that day, and there was only one table left available—the last table. Who knew that over ten years later, we would still be sitting at a table together. We talked and laughed throughout the meal until everyone had finished eating. That's when I snuck inside and brought out Suzie's cake. They all whooped with excitement.

I shushed the group and said, "I need y'all's help with something."

"We'll do anything you want if you give us a piece of that cake," Stephanie replied.

"Anything?" I asked, looking from one to the other.

"Yes. Yes. Anything," they each answered.

"I need you to help me move all my stuff into my new apartment."

Confusion spread across their faces, so I pointed to the garage apartment. "It's right there. I'm moving home."

They surrounded me, hugging my neck excitedly.

"We are all going to be back together again!" Agnes exclaimed.

Latrice piped in, "It's about time. We were wondering how much longer you were going to stay up north."

"We're so happy. We've missed you so much," Kathleen added.

I set the cake onto the table and cut it into six huge slices. "I don't have cake plates or forks, so everyone grab a slice." As they each reached in, I announced, "I'd like to make a toast. To my amazing grandfather, who showed me how to love art. To the talented Suzie, who makes the best damn pound cake in the South. And to my best friends, thank you for loving me from afar until I found my way back home. To the tribe!"

Everyone held up their chunks of cake and tapped them together before taking bites.

The sound of a large gasp turned everyone's head toward the kitchen door. "Janine Therese, is that Suzie's cake?" my mom yelled, before quickly shutting the door behind her to walk onto the porch. "And you're all eating it like animals.

What is wrong with you girls?" she added. We all froze like deer in headlights as she walked to my side, then whispered, "You better give me a bite, you naughty girl."

———

My move-in party with my friends lasted less than thirty minutes. "Just set the boxes over in that corner until I find the right place for everything," I told them. As my eyes swept across the small pile, representing seven years in New York, I began to cry. "That's sad, isn't it?" I said to the group.

Maggie was the first at my side. "Oh, honey, don't be sad. This isn't the end, it's the beginning. And you're not supposed to begin with lots of stuff holding you down."

The room was quiet, but I felt everyone's concerned eyes on me. Latrice was the first one to break the silence. "Damn, Maggie, that was good. Can I schedule my therapy session?"

Everyone laughed, grateful the mood had changed. Kathleen came to stand on my other side. "Now that the boxes are up, can you give us a quick tour before we have to leave?"

"Absolutely," I answered and proceeded to escort them through the kitchen, living room, bathroom, bedroom, then back to the doorway, all in about thirty steps. "Oh, I forgot to tell you the best part of renting this apartment, it comes with three meals a day."

"Oh, wow! Can we rent a room, too? Your mom is such a great cook," Stephanie added.

"I know, right? Now I just need to find a part-time job."

Maggie piped up. "All my kayak instructors have left to go back to college. Rude, I know. The Girl Scouts have tours lined up every weekend for a while. Any interest in working for me on your weekends?"

I carefully answered so as not to sound ungrateful. "Thank

you, Maggie, but I really need to be sketching on my weekends and finding a place that will agree to sell my art."

Agnes jumped in quickly. "Hey, how about Aggies? You could have art shows sometimes in the evenings when we are closed, and I could hang your art that's for sale around the café. It sure would give some color to my walls."

I thought for a moment and could picture my art in her lovely café. "That would be amazing, Agnes. Thank you!"

"Then it's settled." Agnes nodded.

"You guys have solved all my problems in just thirty minutes. Thank you."

The six friends gathered around the doorway, smiling triumphantly. That's how it had always been with the tribe; we could figure out almost any problem when all six of us put our heads together. They each kissed my cheek on their way out and offered their condolences for my grandfather one last time. As I shut the door, I could picture my new life. I had a blank page. I could fill it with anything I'd like, and I couldn't wait to begin.

Chapter 4

The Greatest Gift

Before unpacking, I dove back into my grandfather's closet. Running my hand along the stacks of sketchpads, my eyes focused on a very familiar one. Pulling it from the stack, I sat right down on the floor and tumbled back into my childhood.

My life as an artist began the moment my grandfather gave me that sketchpad. I had never been close to him; he was always lost in his thoughts and had never shown me much attention. Maybe, he just didn't find me interesting enough. But that one summer, he had given me the greatest gift of my young life, a sketchpad and pencils.

My parents had gone on another trip. They had become more frequent since my mother's cookbooks had become popular. Every year, she would search the world for a new flair for her dishes, then practice them on me. I didn't mind, I loved her meals. But more than that, I loved hearing the stories behind where the meals had originated. Her trips were usually a couple of weeks long, and that's when I got to know my grandfather better.

The first few days always went off without a hitch. Grandfather Gerard went his way and I went mine. We only met for meals and sometimes not even then. He definitely wasn't a man on a schedule. He only ate his meals when he was hungry. "We should eat to live, not live to eat," was his motto. Strange that his only child made her living on people craving the complete opposite.

I was surprised one particular morning to hear him calling for me from the bottom of the stairs.

"Janine? Ja Neen?"

I cringed. I hated that name more than anything. Still, it was the name every teacher called out for attendance and every doctor's office had on file for me. I sat quietly. Maybe he would think I was asleep and would go away.

"Janine? Answer please!" he called out again, his long-ago French accent creeping up the stairs.

I got up from the window seat where I had found refuge the last couple of days, placed the book stretched open on my twin bed, to keep my place, and walked to the top of the stairs. "Yes sir?"

"Come down please. We are going on a walk."

I groaned inwardly, then answered, "Coming."

He waited at the door as I awkwardly clambered down the stairs. His dark eyes stared blankly as I approached, then he turned the darkened brass handle and walked out the front door without saying a word. I obediently followed behind.

He carried a backpack and although he was using a walking stick, he seemed to be moving very quickly down the front walkway. When we reached the sidewalk that ran throughout the neighborhood, he motioned for me to walk beside him. I'm not sure if it was being outside or the fact that he didn't have to look me in the eyes, but he began to talk to me. I wasn't expecting it, so I jumped when he began, "Gordonston was the first neighborhood in Savannah, named after an innovative man named William Gordon. I was lucky that your grandmother and I were able to raise our daughter, your mother, here."

Pointing across the street, he said, "I helped your mom build a tree fort in the old oak right there. You can still see the boards."

I nodded, as I tried to picture my mom as a child.

"I taught her to ride a bike right there on that sidewalk," he added as he continued to walk, unraveling the stories from his early years of parenting, reliving them with me. It was almost as if he were a different person, unreserved and carefree.

"And see that park up ahead, that's Juliette Gordon Lowe Park. Remember? I told you about her. She started the Girl Scouts of America. Mr. Gordon, that I told you about, was her grandfather." We walked and he talked right up until we arrived at the park's gate. He quieted down, almost reverently, as he pushed open the iron gate and walked silently to its center, where there was a covered pavilion. I immediately missed the sound of his voice, which surprised me. Placing his bag on one of the picnic tables, he asked me to take a seat.

"I've got something for you," he said, reaching deep into his bag.

I was surprised when he handed me a sketchpad and a pack of charcoal pencils. He then pulled out his own pad and pencils. "I've got one, too," he explained. The only difference was that his held many sketches inside and his pencils were dull. "I thought we could sketch a bit today," he said casually. I must have looked at him strangely because he laughed.

"Don't worry. We're just having a little fun. Anything you draw is perfect," he added.

I nodded and felt a smile slowly turn my lips. When I opened the pencils, the smell of coal filled my nose. I lifted them closer to inhale.

He laughed again. "I do that, too, with new pencils," he said. Leaning over, he breathed in the scent and smiled. "Enjoy," he added before turning and finding a seat on a nearby bench.

Opening the sketchpad, I let my fingers run the length of the page. I closed my eyes and listened to the sound it made as I felt my smile grow larger. When I opened my eyes, I found him watching me.

"We will stay in the park until you're ready to go; you can wander anywhere inside the fence," he explained.

"Yes, sir." I picked up my pad and ran off to begin my first full day of being an artist. *It's hard to believe that was almost twenty years ago,* I thought as I flipped slowly through my old sketchbook. The pictures were not good, but my strokes were strong. Some darker from more pressure, some as faint as the air. He obviously saw something in me to have kept them all of these years. I took my time, flipping through each page, until I turned to the end. Tucked in the back of the book was a torn-off page with a very advanced drawing. I pulled it closer, studying every detail. Seeing, through his eyes, what he saw. It was of me, that very day in the park. I was drawing in a sketchbook that was way too large to be sitting on my lap. But the most beautiful thing in the sketch was the smile on my face. *Pure joy* were the only words to describe it.

I carefully pulled the sketch from the book. *It's time for me to find that joy again. It's time to find my light!*

Chapter 5

The Studio

Luke rubbed his hand down his face, trying hard to focus on his task at hand. "Today's the day," he mumbled. "No more putting this off." He stared over at her studio, knowing how hard this would be. He had avoided things that made him think of Eliana for so long, including the one part of their house that Luke had never felt welcome in—her studio.

Most days, he would stay away from that side of the house completely. But the days he missed her the most, he would wander over to the fountain. The fountain was his happy connection to her ghost. It had been their Switzerland in the last few months of their marriage. Their day-to-day life consisted of the needed conversations that most married couples have, but when they were at the fountain, their conversations came alive. They would arrange to meet there every couple of days to talk. They had decided to leave all negativity away from that space. It was neutral territory. "No fighting, no accusing, and no judgment," Eliana would say, and Luke would comply. Their conversations were mutually intriguing; each challenged the other with their wit. She was his equal match and their happy sparring fueled each of their creativity. He had clung to those times. They reminded him of their earlier years together.

As he sat at the fountain, that warm day in May, he recalled his favorite memory of her.

He had woken up early that morning and realized Eliana wasn't in bed. It wasn't an unusual occurrence. She went to her studio whenever creativity called, day or night. In fact, she had Jorge assemble a small twin bed for those nights so that she wouldn't disturb Luke on her return. That morning, Luke had decided to get up and go to the fountain where he could watch the sun rise over Paris. The city lit up as soon as the sun began to creep into the sky. Brilliant hues of purple and pink seemed to sparkle through the spray of the fountain. He had been deep in thought and had let his eyes settle on the studio door. He could almost picture her asleep on the small makeshift bed and wondered if he should awaken her to show her the beautiful sunrise. That's when he noticed the door slowly opening. Eliana had peeked around, looking for him. She had beamed when their eyes met and had walked toward him. She didn't try to primp her hair or hide the fact that she was wearing one of his old button-downs that was now stained with paint. She had never been embarrassed by her outward imperfections. It was her inner struggles she worked so hard to hide. Her smile became lopsided as she tugged on her lip. Oh, those lips. He stood at her approach and took her into his arms. She was the most beautiful and complicated creature he had ever known, and even though he knew they were trapped in a marriage that was far from normal, he loved her. He had entered into that sacrament with his whole heart and knew that it meant till death do us part.

He found it strange how he could recall that day at the fountain like it had happened yesterday, but it had been years. He could still smell her perfume and sometimes could almost picture her peeking around the door opening, looking for him. But her ghost wouldn't need to peek today; he was going inside.

He stood abruptly and crossed the courtyard in a split second. He only paused for a moment before flinging the door open, but suddenly became scared to cross the threshold. *I'm invading her space,* he thought. That's the moment he saw it— the most exquisite piece of art he'd ever encountered. All reservations disappeared. A force of its own pulled him toward it. It was of a young woman, reaching toward the painter, opening herself up to love. Luke immediately recognized the young woman in the picture. He had seen her firsthand. She had reached for him that day at the fountain with that same expression on her face; the same tug of her lip. He yearned to be a part of this painting, to feel his wife against him again.

Tears streamed down his face as his world began to swim. This happy memory from his past danced with the pain of an aching heart. He needed to sit for a moment, so he eased into a nearby armchair. Closing his eyes, he took a deep breath and continued a slow intake of oxygen until he felt steady. When he opened his eyes, he noticed another painting between the windows. He stood to get a better look when he noticed another one blocking the fireplace, and one more sitting on an easel. Each one was magnificent. She had painted four perfect masterpieces. His jaw tightened. Why hadn't she shared them with him? He had been to her studio numerous times. Where had Eliana hidden these? Sadness gripped him while his brain searched for answers. These beautiful paintings had just been sitting in her studio for a year.

Luke's confusion was overwhelming. He had to get out of there. He ran back out to the fountain—to Switzerland. But once he was there, he knew it would never be neutral territory again. How could she be neutral? She must have hated him. If not, she would have let him into her world.

He had known she was a passionate artist when they had met. He had loved that about her. He even thought he could watch and learn from her, but her superb skill and his mediocrity created a wedge. Still, his paintings were good and he wanted to show them. He tried to talk Eliana into opening a gallery to show both of their works, but she was uninterested. She did, however, encourage him to move forward in opening a gallery. In fact, at times, it felt like she over-encouraged. He began to believe she wanted him to be distracted, so that she could be alone in her studio, doing the one thing that meant more to her than anything or anyone else, painting. If that was the case, she definitely got her wish.

She listened to all his plans and offered great suggestions for the studio. Her family was well-known in the art community, so they used her maiden name and named it Gallery Laroche. He found the perfect location on Rue des Trois Freres Street at a place he named Five Points, where he could reach locals and tourists and create a space to support the community. He hired a diverse staff who were able to do everything from offering art classes to orchestrating first-class exhibitions. He was also able to showcase his latest work. That is when Renae approached him.

Renae was an agent who went to great lengths to get an interview with him. She lathered him with compliments about the gallery, but then explained that in order to survive, people in the art world needed to know his name. He hired her on the spot and she delivered everything she promised. Both his name and his art became recognized in Paris. People began to take him seriously and many artists began asking him for studio showings. Renae was smart, but she had an edge to her that made him uncomfortable, especially when she began asking for meetings with Eliana.

Chapter 6

Announcements

Savannah, Georgia

It had been nearly four years since I had taken the time to walk inside the Gordonston garden, although I passed it every day. Somehow, it felt like something from my past, so I had stayed away, until today.

He should be here, I thought. He would want to celebrate this moment with me. This was as much his as it was mine. I half-heartedly picked up my art school graduation announcements after my last class, not sure if I would even attend. I was almost ten years older than most of my class. Still, I never felt the gap until we were together as a whole class. In the last year, most of my days were spent alone, and I preferred it that way.

I moved slowly to the spot and stopped just before I reached his marker. Kneeling down, I pulled the long piece of centipede grass that had run across the round piece of concrete, then swept the stone with my hand. Smiling, I thought back to the day I had found it, a few weeks after I moved back home. Taking my index finger, I followed the writing he had chiseled into the twelve-inch stone. "Find Your Light."

Over those years, I did find my light, lost it, and found it again. An artist's creativity peaks and wanes. That's a little tidbit my grandfather forgot to share. Still, I had completed art school and I knew it would have made him happy.

I glanced down at my announcement. Other than my parents, there were only six people I wanted to share my good news with. I would be having lunch with five of them this afternoon, but the sixth invitation would remain here, with the person who opened the world of art to me. I tucked it under the corner of the stone, said a quick prayer and scurried off to deliver the next five announcements.

———

As soon as I walked through the door of the famous Italian restaurant on Congress Street, my mood lifted. The smell of garlic spun around the darkened room. I waited in the foyer for my eyes to adjust as the hostess welcomed me.

"I'm meeting my friends," I explained as I spotted the group sitting under one of the large cafe umbrellas scattered around the dining room. The restaurant decorated each one with a string of lights. Paired with the low lighting, it gave the appearance of having dinner at an outdoor cafe in Italy, no matter the time of day.

As I approached the table, I quickly pulled out the invitations from my bag. I walked around the table, leaving one on each of their plates while calling them each by name. "Agnes. Kathleen. Latrice. Stephanie. Maggie."

They excitedly opened their envelopes and responded together in a large roar of excitement.

"You did it, and you finished early. We're so proud of you," Kathleen said, speaking for the group.

I shrugged my shoulders. "I guess it's official."

"It was official the moment you picked up a sketchpad. I sure love that story about your grandfather giving it to you," Latrice commented. "I know he would have been in the front row."

"Well, he would have been there alone. I'm not going," I shared with the group.

"Oh, yes you are going," Stephanie chided. "You worked too hard not to celebrate this achievement."

I rolled my eyes and answered, "I'm literally the oldest person in my class. Hell, I think a few of the teachers are younger than I am. How embarrassing."

"Embarrassing? You're famous. You've got a string of people in line for their next commissioned piece," Latrice added.

"I'm not famous," I responded, shaking my head at the absurdity of it all.

Maggie quickly added, "Maybe not famous like that fancy-schmancy, big-wig artist I heard is giving the commencement address, but you're famous in Savannah."

"His name is Luke Dupris. He would be the one and only reason I would go to the ceremony," I added.

"So, you're going?" Kathleen asked.

I looked around the table at my five best friends. Each of us was so different, but we loved one another through every up and down. They were waiting for my response. "Yes. I guess I'll go."

The table cheered, and Kathleen added, once again speaking for the group, "Then so will we! RSVP for five, please."

Chapter 7

The Imposter

Montmartre, France

"We've been very successful releasing three paintings spread out over four years. What a shame this is the last one," Renae commented as she studied each stroke on the canvas. "Your wife was unbelievably talented."

Luke stood beside his agent, inspecting the masterpiece. "She named this one herself. The back of the canvas reads *Mount of Martyrs*."

"*Mount of Martyrs*. It's funny she didn't just name it *Montmartre*, since that's what it means. Still, it's very sweet she dedicated it to her home city."

"I'm not so sure about that. I believe she dedicated this one to Saint Denis since he was the actual martyr this area is named after." Luke focused on a figure in the painting and commented further. "And look at this woman in the background. Doesn't she have an uncanny resemblance to Eliana?"

Renae shook her head slowly as she examined it more

closely. "I don't see it. But that's the beauty of this fine piece of art, it has many meanings."

Luke nodded in agreement, knowing in his heart that he was right. He and Eliana had many discussions about her faith. She spoke about the patron saint of France often. His execution felt almost personal to her. But she always ended her story saying that he got the last laugh. After they beheaded Saint Dennis, the first bishop of Paris picked up his head and walked several miles preaching to all who looked on.

Luke stared at the figure his wife had painted that looked so much like herself. He was so deep in thought, he didn't hear Renae calling his name.

"Hello? Hello? Anyone home?" she teased as she waved her hand in front of his face.

Luke shook his head as he refocused. "So sorry. What were you saying?"

"A name. Do you want to use the name she gave it? I know you named the other three."

He cleared his throat. "*Montmartre*. Let's name it *Montmartre*. It sounds much more romantic than *Martyr's Hill* and yet it means the same thing."

Renae nodded, then slowly began her next sentence. "It's time to talk business. We need to discuss the elephant in the room. This is our last painting. Correction, this is your last painting. Do you have any ideas what comes after this?"

Luke smiled, ever so slightly. "Yes. I've decided I am going to paint the next one myself," he said proudly.

Renae interrupted. "No, you're not. We didn't work this hard for all our secrets to be revealed. The minute you put one of your paintings out, everybody will know."

"You do remember I'm an artist, don't you? You signed me as a client before we ever found these paintings. Before Eliana even died. I think it's time for me to stop pretending I'm somebody else," he replied.

Renae took a deep breath. Lowering her voice, she spoke slowly, as if she were speaking to a child. "I hear you. And yes, you are a wonderful artist. However, when we decided to display Eliana's paintings as your own, we agreed that you would never paint again. People see a progression in your artwork, and no one would believe you could regress in your style. People would start asking questions, and you would be destroyed. That's why you agreed to stop painting—because people would notice."

"When we decided to show Eliana's painting as my own? Don't you mean when you decided? You didn't ask my permission before you made the press release about my new painting, did you?"

Renae held up her hand, "You know that wasn't my fault. I listed the artist just as Eliana signed her picture, as L Depris. I had no idea the world would think the L was for Luke. I thought we moved past this. It does no good to go backwards."

Luke stared at her coldly. He knew in his heart that she had known exactly what she was doing. But he knew that Eliana's paintings needed to be shared with the world; they were too extraordinary to keep to himself. So, he agreed. Looking back, he wished he had gone public after that first press release and told everyone that he had found lost paintings belonging to his wife who had passed away. But he hadn't been prepared when he arrived at his gallery the morning after the announcement. Hundreds of reporters were eagerly waiting for him to address them. Instead, he had waved and nodded and told them thank you. If he was being honest, he loved the recognition. He had worked hard at his gallery and was excited to be in the limelight. His vanity had brought this on himself, and he had to continue to comply.

"Okay, Renae. I understand," Luke mumbled as his gaze fell to the floor.

Renae waited a moment to let the tension clear a bit, then said, "I might have a solution." His eyes slowly moved to hers. He was ready to listen, so she continued. "The Laroche family comes from a long line of artists. We all know the legend about their family being blessed with extraordinary artists. If it's true, then why don't we find another family member to do the next painting?"

Luke answered quickly, "Eliana was the only child of an only child."

"Yes. But her grandfather was not. He had many siblings. I came upon a painting a while back in a gallery with the artists name being G. Laroche. He must have been young when he completed the painting. It was rough, but still exceptional. It wasn't easy, but I tracked him down and understand he immigrated to the U.S."

"And?" Luke asked.

"And he lived in Georgia in a city called Savannah. He recently passed away, but he has family. One of them just happens to be graduating from the exceptional art school in Savannah. So, I reached out to them. I told them you would be in the area for business and that you'd love to give their commencement speech next month."

Luke looked at her in disbelief. "You want me to travel to this Savannah, give a commencement speech, find this young artist, and ask him to paint a picture for me? Why would he ever do that?"

"First of all, the he is a she and is already being recognized for her art. And secondly, since she's still a nobody, I feel quite sure she would love to sell her paintings to a famous painter. We will pay generously," Renae answered.

Luke ran his fingers through his hair. Shaking his head, he

said, "I think I'm done. I'm happy to be out of the spotlight. I have my studio and my community. I don't need this anymore."

"No, but I do," she said with a coldness that surprised Luke. "Do you think people will still come to the studio if they find out you lied all this time? Do you think your precious community will still support you?"

"You would do that to me? After all this time?" Luke whispered, the hurt coming through in his voice.

"I would do it for us, Luke. Both of us lose if we stop." Renae straightened her pinpoint skirt and lifted her chin, before adding, "Do you need my help packing?"

Luke's eyes burned through her. "No," he said through gritted teeth.

"You won't be disappointed. I'll send the arrangements to Christine," she said over her shoulder as she walked out the door.

Luke looked around the studio and let his eyes settle on the figure in Eliana's last painting. The figure he knew to be his late wife. "I'm sorry, Eliana," he whispered. As the words came out of his mouth, he noticed something on the painting for the first time. Hanging around the neck of this figure was a medallion. A medallion he knew too well. The same medallion Eliana wore around her neck and never took off. The same one he buried her still wearing. The Miraculous Medal, silver with a ruby red rim. It was her in the painting. Eliana was trying to tell him something, but what? He knew, at that very moment, he would need to go to Savannah to find her family.

Chapter 8

Finding an Artist

Luke arrived in Savannah the week before he was scheduled to give the art school's commencement speech. He had decided to start at the source and first find the graveside of G. Laroche. He had been easy to find. He was buried in Savannah's Catholic Cemetery. But as Luke stared down at the tombstone, he was surprised by its engraving. It was the picture of the Miraculous Medal—just like every other tombstone in the Laroche cemetery plot in Montmartre. *Did Eliana know she had family living in America?* he wondered, before noticing the fresh flowers on the graves of both Mr. and Mrs. Laroche.

He was happy to see that someone was caring for the plots. He read over the late Mr. Laroche's obituary, which Renae had sent with him, and was able to find the name of his daughter, who lived in Savannah. She now had the last name of Farris. "The cookbook lady. Very interesting," he muttered, remembering he had seen a display of her books at his favorite bookstore in Paris.

After digging a little, he found an address that matched the name, and the next thing you know, he was sitting in front of a two-story house in a neighborhood in Savannah called Gordonston, wondering how to play out his inquisition.

I'll knock on the door and ask for Mr. Laroche. I'll act like I don't know he has passed away, he thought. However, when a middle-aged man answered the door, Luke began to stammer. He finally was able to come up with the statement, "I'm looking for an artist that lives at this address."

The man who had answered the door smiled broadly and stood proudly. "You're at the right place; that would be my daughter, Jan," he replied. Luke stood quietly and was happy when the man continued. "Are you meeting with all the graduates from the art college?"

Luke thought quickly before responding. "No, I'm just informing students of some last-minute job opportunities. We're having a hard time getting in touch with everyone; you know how college graduates are."

The man quickly stepped back from the door, motioning for Luke to come inside. "Job offers? Come in, come in. Jan's not here, but I'm happy to tell her all about them."

Luke smiled and waved off his offer. "Can you please just tell her to get all of her info into the school before graduation tomorrow?"

"Oh, sure thing. I'll make sure to tell her."

Luke retreated quickly, exhaling with a breath of relief when he heard the door close behind him. He jumped into the car, drove around the corner, and pulled the car to a stop. "I'm speaking at Jan's commencement tomorrow," he mumbled to himself. "And if she paints like her relatives, I will have hit the jackpot."

———

I watched my friends walk into the square and scan the graduates looking for me. They looked worried when they couldn't find me and began to look around the square. Their faces lit up when they saw me leaning on the tall oak, away from the group.

The rustle of the leaves above me made it impossible to hear what they were saying to me as they approached. I welcomed the wind on my face. Although it was only May, I was burning up. I had found refuge in the shade of the tall oak.

"Well, don't you all look nice," I said as they gathered around me, each fighting for their own plot of shade. They were wearing sundresses that were vibrant in color, which had probably been bought brand new for Easter. They looked summery and cool, a drastic contrast to my black cap and gown.

The sun seemed to disappear in an instant as the breeze blew through once again, this time with more strength. Kathleen reached up just in time to catch her straw hat as the bottom of Stephanie's dress was blown straight up to her waist. We all cried out and turned to the commotion in the square as two of the tents took flight.

Within seconds, a voice came over a megaphone asking the graduates to quickly make our way into the Student Center and asking the guests to please leave the square. Everyone scurried in different directions as the sky blackened.

"Graduates, please find a place along the corridor," a voice cried out over the megaphone as my class found refuge inside the building.

The storm had come out of nowhere. The sound of thunder now echoed down the hallway, hurting my ears. The building shook around me like a shock wave. *These Savanah Grey bricks have withstood storms for hundreds of years; I'm sure I'll be fine,* I told myself. The electricity cracked, then immediately popped off.

I shook my head. The committee had worked so hard decorating the square and setting up the tents and chairs. It really was a shame for the graduates who had been waiting for this day for so long. I was different. Being older, and possibly a little wiser, I had been working as an artist for years. I began to wonder if the storm was a sign from above for me not to participate. But fate had another plan.

"Attention, graduates," came the voice over the megaphone again. "We will proceed with the graduation." Everyone around me whooped excitedly. Everyone except me. The announcer continued. "We've moved the ceremony inside to the auditorium. I'm sorry to tell you that it will not hold all of those who had turned out in the park. We're allowing parents only. Sorry for any inconvenience."

The thunder boomed again, quieting the hallway. I couldn't believe this. I didn't want to be here in the first place. Couldn't they just move along the hall and hand us our damn diplomas?

A strong, male voice rang out down the corridor. "Please stay in place. Your parents are being escorted into the auditorium as we locate candles for each of you to carry into graduation. This year will surely be memorable." The man's strong Southern accent made me smile. I could almost picture him standing there in his summer suit. If nothing else, Savannah's Art College could always put on a good show.

I slid down to the floor and leaned against the wall. When I moved my small handbag closer, I felt the beautiful silver flask that the tribe had given me for graduation. Running my fingers over the monogram on the front, I traced my initials in the darkness and thought about them giving it to me the week prior.

"It's pre-filled with peppermint schnapps, because we know it's your favorite," Latrice had explained.

"And it's monogrammed, so it won't get mixed up with any of our flasks," Agnes added.

"It can only be used in celebration," Stephanie remarked.

"And never drink alone," Maggie had chimed in.

"Because you always, and I mean always, have us. We are so proud of you, Jan," Kathleen finished.

Tears stung my eyes. I was so sad my friends wouldn't be at my graduation. I held up the flask to the long, dark hallway and announced, "I'm celebrating with all my fellow graduates. Cheers, graduates."

The schnapps burned its way down to my belly. I began to put the top on the flask when a male's voice beside me asked. "Hey, can I have a swig?"

"Sure. We're all celebrating. Congratulations," I said, passing it through the darkness in his direction.

As our hands touched, he said, "I'm 21, so we're good."

I groaned loudly, then kiddingly said, "Take only one sip or I'll have to tell the principal." I was surprised when he answered, "Yes, ma'am."

We were interrupted by the megaphone. "It's showtime. Stay in line walking into the auditorium. I know you are upset that all your family and friends aren't here, but we will be videotaping the whole ceremony so you can share it with your loved ones at a later time.

Is that supposed to make me happy? I wondered.

The ceremony went more smoothly than anticipated until it was my turn to receive my diploma. I had practiced numerous times outside. Still, on my way back to my seat, the indoor darkness hid the top stair and I fell all the way to the bottom. Thankfully, most people didn't see it because of the darkness. At least, that's what I thought.

Chapter 9

The Dive

I hobbled the several blocks toward my car. My leg had finally stopped bleeding from my fall, but I was in pain. When I looked up and saw the Pinkie Masters sign, I knew what would take the pain away.

Pinkie's is a corner bar where you could blend in and never need to get involved in conversation, unless you wanted to. I checked my wallet to make sure I had cash, because Pinkies doesn't take cards. Luckily, I found a ten floating in the side pocket, so I went inside.

After ordering a beer, I found a table away from the bar and began to doodle on a bar napkin. I had always been like that; anything was my canvas. I drew a border around the edges, then began to fill in the center as the figure of Saint Michael began to take shape.

I felt a man's presence as he sat down across from me, but I was completely focused on my drawing and didn't want to be interrupted tonight by one of Pinkie's regulars.

"Go away," I muttered. I continued scribbling until I completed the wing of my drawing, only glancing up when he stood and walked around the table to observe. I stopped, pen in midair, and just stared.

He began, "I'm…"

I cut him off. "I know who you are."

"Yes, I guess you would," he answered.

I waited for him to speak, but he only stared. *Why is he staring at me like that?* I finally asked, "Uh, can I help you with something?"

He nodded. "It's Jan, right?"

I tried to hide my surprise, nervously taking a sip of my beer.

He continued, "I saw some of your work displayed at the college. I'm impressed."

How can he be impressed by me? I watched as a drop of water dripped from the bottom of my beer bottle. The second the liquid hit the paper napkin, the ink began to spread. He reached out to try to save it as I swiped it into a ball.

"What a shame. Saint Michael the Archangel defends us in battle," he muttered. "Profound, but true."

"Should I be preparing for battle?" I asked, watching his face process my statement. Our eyes met, but I didn't look away. Something about him made me nervous, but I was also drawn to his intensity.

"You just graduated from art school. Why do you look so down?" he asked.

I took another sip of beer. Tilting my head, I looked him over, then looked past him to see if he was alone. "Why would a world-renowned artist whose face is on every magazine around the world find themselves in this dive bar talking to a pion artist like me?"

He smiled. It surprised me. Not only by the fact that he offered me a smile, but also by the way it made my stomach flip.

"What's your 'what's next,' Jan?"

I was quiet, contemplating how to answer. "I have commissioned art requests from people all over the South, but..." *Why did I add "but?* I wasn't sure how to finish my sentence. He sat quietly, almost knowingly, waiting for my mind to comprehend what my heart already knew. I turned up the last of my beer, then finished my sentence. "But I think I need a break before I begin the rest of my life."

Again, the smile. "Come to Paris."

"Yeah, right," I muttered, expecting him to realize I wasn't worth the effort and leave. But somewhere, deep in my soul, I was hoping he wouldn't. Could he truly be that interested?

"Come to Paris, with me."

I shook my head. "I know you're probably used to women falling at your feet, but I've had enough of these beers to speak my mind, and I'm not that kind of girl."

His laugh quieted the bar. "This is not a proposition; it's an opportunity."

I studied him and smiled when he squirmed. "What's in it for you?"

He seemed taken aback, probably not used to people questioning him. "You're the most successful artist in the world and old enough to be my dad. Why would you want me to come to Paris with you?"

He pulled his chair closer. Leaning in, he whispered, "I'm in a slump."

"Yeah, right."

"Everyone sees only what I want them to see. I'm in a slump, and for the first time in my life, I'm scared. I walked into this dive bar tonight, and I see you scribbling on a napkin like I once did. Like if you weren't drawing, you'd die. I had seen your name on incredible art at the college. Then I realized you were the woman behind it at the ceremony today. You made quite an exit, too."

I smiled but suddenly felt the pain in my hip from the fall. I rubbed my leg, then turned my attention back to him.

"You're good. But you have a lot to learn. Paris can give you that, and I can stick close to your side, hoping some of your passion will rub off on me."

I gave him a dead stare.

He quickly added, "Passion for art. Passion for life. Not passion for me."

I began nodding slowly until he added, "Still, I assure you, I'm nowhere near the age of your dad."

I looked around the bar until my eyes fell to the napkin. *I've always wanted to go to France, and good gosh, I'm being asked by Luke Depris. What am I, crazy?* Looking up, I met his stare. "When would we leave?"

Glancing at his watch, he answered, "In seven hours. The plane won't wait."

I nodded only once. "I'll be there."

"I'll have a car waiting in front of your house at five a.m. *Bonsoir,* Jan," he whispered, and left before hearing my reply.

———

LUKE WAS READY TO BE BACK IN HIS HOME IN Montmartre, although Savannah had surprised him with its charm. He had stayed in a quaint inn in the historic district that was only two blocks from the famous Forsyth Park. His room was cozy, with a relaxing outdoor spa feature, but the best part about his stay was that no one knew him. He was just Luke from France.

The inn's owners had given him several tips on where to eat and what to see. He had checked off most of them, but he found his favorite quickly—Savannah's beach, Tybee. He had driven down to the small seaside town twice. The first time, he had only allowed himself a couple of hours and he ran out of time. On the drive back to the inn that afternoon, he had rolled down his windows and smelled the acrid mud along the marsh-lined road just as the sun was setting. It brought him such a complete feeling of peace that he made the time to ride down to the beach a second time before leaving.

It was on that trip that he fell in love with this small island sitting on the Atlantic Ocean. Its pace. The friendly locals. And it's beauty. In all his travels around the world, there were only a handful of places that he felt he could actually make his residence. Tybee Island was one of those places.

But for now, he had a job to finish. He'd almost finished what he had come for. He had gone to the college the day before to practice his speech, and while there, he had asked the college if they'd share the address of Jan Farris because he was looking for an intern and thought her work would be perfect. What they didn't know was that he had not seen any of her work at that time and was going by Renae's recommendation to find a family member.

That night after graduation, she had disappeared before he had gotten the chance to meet her, probably embarrassed by her fall down the stairs. He was shocked to find her in the little dive bar he had ducked into that afternoon. What were the odds? It must have been meant to be.

It was unsettling to him how much she looked like his wife. Although where his wife had been plain, this young lady was attractive. Still, they shared similar features—one in particular had unnerved him. Her lips. She had Eliane's lips. She pursed them and tugged on them so many times during their conversation. It had tortured him. He hadn't expected to feel attracted to her, and maybe that wasn't exactly what he was feeling. But something was there that he hadn't been prepared for. He was just doing the job that needed to be done. But as he walked back to his hotel room, he found himself thinking about her and wanting to know more about her. Nothing good could come from that.

It's probably just this warm Southern air playing tricks on my mind, he thought. He wasn't sure. For the first time in a very long time, he felt excited by the unknown and anticipated the several weeks ahead.

Chapter 10

Departure

I felt guilty leaving my parents a note like this. I would have told them when I got in last night. I had looked up at their bedroom window to see if they were awake, but their lights were off. I knew better than to wake them. Besides, I was an adult now; they'll be fine. Shrugging, I scanned the kitchen for the pad of paper they always left on the table for their running grocery list. Grabbing a pen, I sat down and began to write.

Dear Mom and Dad,

I found out late last night that I was awarded an art apprenticeship with Luke Depris. The only downside was that his plane was leaving first thing this morning. Looks like I'm going to Paris. Hooray! I'll call you once I settle in.

I love you, Jan

. . .

P.S. – I have no idea how long that will be. I stacked my stuff
in the corner of the apartment. I understand if you would like
to rent it while I'm gone.

I STARED DOWN AT THE LETTER. *I SHOULD WAKE THEM.*
Yeah, I should totally wake them. I checked the time and realized the car should be pulling up any minute. I didn't have time
for their questions. I had taken the cowardly way out and no
longer had time to fix it. Plus, I had lied. An art apprenticeship
program? There was no such thing. *I'm just a young, naïve*
artist going to Paris with a total stranger to...to...what? I can't
even answer that question. Thank heavens my parents were still
asleep. They could smell a lie a mile away and would talk me
out of going.

Still, I felt guilty. I pulled the letter back in front of me and
added:

P.S.S. - Thank you for coming to my graduation and always
supporting my art. I couldn't ask for better parents. I hope I
make y'all proud.

————

I SLUNK DOWN THE WALKWAY LIKE A TEENAGER SNEAKING
out to a party. I had nothing to be ashamed of. I was a grown
woman. I lived in New York for years. Truth be known, I
should feel guilty for that time—not now. But, since I moved
back to Savannah four years ago, I decided to try and shape up.
I wanted to be a better daughter, a better artist, a better person.

But my desire for adventure outweighed all of that. *I'm going to Paris, dammit. No guilt.*

THE CAR WAITING AT THE CURB WAS DARK AND SLEEK. As I approached, the passenger door opened and a young woman stepped out. I paused. She was about my age, sleek, and dressed in a business pantsuit. Her short hair softened her face and showed off her plunging neckline. I instantly felt like a slob in my jeans. However, I would have felt that way no matter what I was wearing.

The woman looked me over, rolled her eyes, and motioned for me to hurry along. As I got closer, she introduced herself. "I'm Christine. We must be going. Put your bags in the trunk and get in please."

I opened my mouth to introduce myself, but she had already turned and was climbing back into the car. I threw my bags in the trunk, closed it and hopped in the back seat to find I was alone. The car pulled off as soon as I shut the door and I became the audience to Christine and the driver's conversation, all in French. The driver glanced at me in his rearview mirror, made a comment to Christine and they both laughed.

I wanted to engage the two of them, so the next time the driver turned his attention to me, I quickly said, "Thank you for picking me up." He offered me a quick nod before moving his eyes to the road ahead.

I continued to try to be a part of their conversation by asking a direct question. "What time is our flight, Christine?"

The conversation stopped as Christine slightly turned her head toward the backseat. "Seven twenty," she said curtly, with her heavy accent before turning her head away. This time, the two of them spoke quietly to one another.

I turned my attention out the window as the car moved down the streets of my Gordonston neighborhood. The oak-covered sidewalks showed the age of the houses, which were said to be part of the oldest neighborhood in Savannah. They turned onto Pennsylvania Avenue, then onto the Island's Expressway. I watched the blur of buildings as they passed. My eyes became heavy. A lot had happened in the past seven hours, and I had barely slept a wink. I snuggled my head into a spot between the car window and my bunched-up purse and fell into a deep sleep.

The next thing I knew, I was falling. I hit the pavement hard. My head jerked up and my heart hammered in my chest as I tried to get my bearings and catch my breath, but I was only met by the sound of Christine's laugh. I jumped into a standing position quickly, found the source of the laughter, and got in her face. My actions stunned her to silence; bullies were usually like that. "Who in the hell do you think you are? You DON'T want to mess with me, I assure you!" I warned.

Christine took one step back. "Oo la la. The sweet little artist has a bite. You're not like the others," she said with a smirk. Still, her eyes showed respect that hadn't been there before. "Come, let me help you," she added, as she knelt on the ground.

I looked down at the content of my purse, scattered on the ground. My makeshift pillow had exploded when the door opened. Christine began stuffing random items back into my bag. I nodded with appreciation and joined in. We both crawled along the sidewalk replacing the contents of my purse. I screamed as Christine began to put in the last item. "Stop. That doesn't belong to me!"

"*Merde!*" Christine yelled out as the small, blue hairbrush that needed to be cleaned, fell to the ground.

We began to laugh and continued to giggle all the way into the terminal. We hurried to the gate and arrived just as the plane began to board. Luke was waiting. He caught her eye and waved as he continued to walk in with the first-class passengers. Christine turned to me and said, "I'm sorry. I didn't know I'd like you when I booked your flight late last night."

"Sorry? For what?"

"You'll see. I've got to go. You wait here until they call your section." She left me and pushed her way to the front of the line, disappearing down the jetway.

I checked my zone, basic economy. *I'm going to Paris. I really don't care if I am in the very last seat beside the bathroom.* Or so I thought.

Chapter 11

The Terminal

The first leg of our flight landed in Atlanta. When I exited the plane, I was met by an airline employee who ushered me to the second flight terminal. "Mr. Dupris didn't want to be crowded by fans, so he asked me to escort you," he explained. I was taken to the international terminal and shown where my next flight would depart from, but there was no one there. Where did everyone go? Then I realized I had five hours to wait, so I wandered the terminal, grabbed a burger and bought a book while I waited.

As the time drew near, I noticed Luke pass once again. He searched the crowd until our eyes met. He mouthed, "You okay?" I gave him a thumbs up and he proceeded onto the plane, followed by Christine.

Thirty minutes later, I found my seat in the very back row. I was in the middle seat, wedged in the center of four other travelers, directly in front of the bathroom. Christine was correct; it was the worst seat on the plane.

I stepped across two women before collapsing into my seat and practically into the lap of the young man in the next seat.

He must have heard the grunts from the two passengers I had ungracefully passed, so he had scooted as far as he could, either to give me more room or to try to get away from me. Regardless, I was grateful.

As soon as he heard the click of my seatbelt, he leaned over slightly and said, "Business or pleasure?"

I turned toward him to see the side of his face. "That's a good question. I guess, a bit of both," I answered while continuing to look in his direction. *I know him*, I thought. *But how? Even his voice sounds familiar.* But I couldn't place him, so I asked, "How about you?"

He smiled. "Definitely business."

We made it through introductions. His name was Eddie and he lived in Tennessee. He played the guitar in various bands, one that I had actually seen in Savannah's Battle of the Bands. That's how I recognized him. Now he was filling in for the guitarist in a band called The Punks as they toured France. I told him I was an artist who had just graduated and had been offered an art internship in France. It was funny how that lie was spilling out so easily since I told it the first time. I almost believed it myself.

We were interrupted by the drink cart. I was surprised when he ordered two cocktails. "It takes a long time for them to come back around," he explained. I followed his lead. "Two screwdrivers, please," I said to the attendant when it became my turn. I heard him snicker.

Four empty glasses later, I had told him my whole life story, even the dark and ugly parts from New York. There's something about meeting people on a plane. Fate has you traveling to the same destination but knowing you will never see them again gives you the freedom to say almost anything.

He had a husky voice and a contagious laugh. It was hard to look him in the face since he was sitting so close, but I couldn't take my eyes off his hands. I'd never noticed a man's hands before, which actually surprised me. Being an artist, hands should always catch my eye. But the best thing about his hands was that they were free of a wedding band.

He was thirty and had been a musician basically since birth. He grew up in Statesboro, home to the Georgia Southern Eagles, but had moved to Nashville to pursue a music career. It was there that an agent signed him and found him many jobs, the latest one was being a summer replacement for the guitarist in The Punks while they were on a year-long tour of France.

We were deep in conversation when I heard my name. I turned and looked into the very serious face of Luke. He motioned with his head and said, "Come with me."

Eddie leaned in closer to me. "Is that your dad?"

I giggled as a flashback of Luke telling me he was nowhere near my dad's age flashed in my mind.

"No, but it looks like I've got to go," I answered as I began to stand.

Eddie touched my arm so I turned his way. "I enjoyed talking with you, Jan," he said

"Me, too. Bye, Eddie," I said to my new friend, making my way toward the aisle before following Luke toward the front of the plane.

As we settled into the large, comfy seats in first class, Luke explained that Christine had purchased the wrong ticket. So, when he saw an open seat, he upgraded me.

I thanked him and then surveyed my surroundings, finding a pouch with items I might need: an eye mask, headphones, a blanket and even a toothbrush. A stewardess approached me and offered me a warm towel that smelled like Eucalyptus. I laughed at the absurdity of it all. Five minutes before, I was surrounded by the smell of airplane lavatories, and now I was patting my face with a warm spa towel.

"May I offer you a beverage?" she then asked.

I thought about Eddie saying to order two since they seldom came around, so I replied, "I'll take two glasses of Champagne."

Luke overheard and must have assumed one of those glasses was for him as he said, "No thanks, I don't care for one."

The stewardess turned back to me. I held up two fingers. She smiled, but it held no warmth.

I drank my first glass as Luke told me about his home on the outskirts of Paris, in Montmartre. My eyes became heavy as the plane flew, crossing many time zones through the night. I listened to his voice, speaking softly, almost reverently, about his home that he called Laroche Château while sipping my second glass. I found it ironic that his house had my grandfather's last name, but I was suddenly too tired to ask questions. I then drifted off to sleep for the rest of the flight.

I was jolted awake when the plane hit the runway. My head was thrust forward as we bounced a few times before the plane slammed on the brakes. I clutched my chest, trying to slow the feeling of my heart beating out of control. Someone should have warned me. I looked to Luke who was calmly reading a magazine. *I'm having a heart attack here, and he's reading a damn magazine?* He didn't say a word to me or anyone else. Once the plane came to a stop, the stewardess approached him and whispered something in his ear. He smiled and she ran her hand down his lapel before turning to the next first-class passenger. I gathered my things quietly, and when he stood to depart the plane, I followed. We walked down the jet bridge, and when we were almost to the terminal gate, I heard someone calling out my name.

"Jan. Hey, Jan. Wait up."

I turned to see Eddie, passing passengers to catch up.

Christine had noticed him as well. "You sure made a good

impression on Mr. Sexy back there," she said out of the side of her mouth.

Suddenly, Luke seemed to find his voice. "We must go; we have a car waiting."

I nodded and continued to walk. But as soon as we were in the terminal, Eddie caught up. I felt his eyes on me before he spoke. I smiled but continued to walk.

"Hey. You okay?" Eddie asked.

This time, Luke stopped and addressed him. "I'm not sure what your aim is here, but the lady is with me. You're making a scene."

Eddie glanced at me, then back to Luke before holding up his hands. Taking a step back, he said, "Listen, man, I'm not trying to get in your business. I just really enjoyed getting to know Jan on the plane. I didn't realize you were together."

Eddie's honesty made me find my voice. I belonged to no one, and I was certainly not with Luke. I reached toward him and placed my hand on his upper arm. "I enjoyed our talk, too, Eddie. I'm here on an internship for the summer, but why don't you look me up when you're back stateside? I'd love to finish our conversation."

The look on Eddie's face completely changed. He turned to me and looked deep in my eyes, like he could read my mind. I watched a smile creep across his face before he said, "I'd really like that." Then, he slowly moved toward me and kissed my cheek. "I look forward to seeing you again," he whispered before wandering off down the terminal.

Chapter 12

Laroche Château

The tapping sound of Luke's wingtip shoes caught my attention. When I turned towards him, he said, "Can we go now?" as if he were addressing a child.

Anger filled me. I'd always done my best to stay away from self-centered people, and here I was in Paris with their king. Sure, I had made him wait while Eddie kissed my cheek, but he could give me those thirty seconds. It wasn't a big deal. I straightened my back and fired off. "Let's get something straight. I don't care how people all over the world treat you, and I don't care that you're paying for me to be in Paris. You asked me here. I am your guest, and you will not be rude to me. Do you understand?"

He rolled his eyes and began to walk off. I didn't budge. Christine shrugged and caught up with him quickly as he continued to walk away. He didn't look back. I stayed firm. Surely, he would at least get Christine to tell me to keep up, but he didn't. *He's going to leave me all alone in this foreign airport.* I quickly gathered my bags, which I had let fall to the ground during our interaction, but when I looked up, I could no longer see them. An announcement came over the intercom in French. My stomach tightened as I began to worry. I didn't even speak their language. I started to run in the direction they had disappeared until I hit a central hub with halls going in every direction. *What do I do?*

Luggage. We had checked luggage that had to be retrieved. I began looking for signs to baggage claim then followed them through Charles de Gaulle airport, each step fueling my fire. As I started walking up to the carousel, I heard my name over the announcement in very broken English. "Paging Jan Farris. Your party is waiting for you at baggage claim. Jan Farris, your party is waiting for you at baggage claim. Then I saw Luke. Relief washed over me—relief and the overwhelming desire to throat-punch him.

As soon as I was within earshot, he called out, "I'm sorry for being rude. It won't happen again." I approached him without taking my eyes off him. *I'm not scared of him. I'm here by choice.* Once we were face-to-face, he nodded and announced, "Welcome to Paris!"

Our car moved at a snail's pace, constantly moving in and out of traffic whenever the driver saw an inch of maneuver room. Thoughts of New York flooded my mind as I stared out the window. Everything was in motion. Since moving back to Savannah four years ago, I had forgotten the hustle and bustle of crowded streets. I felt the tension in my stomach as I worried if I'd be able to jump back into city life. At the same time, I felt a tingle of excitement.

Luke had barely said a word since we left the airport. He was busy, going through papers in a file folder Christine had handed him and asking her questions about each one—in French.

The car continued moving until the traffic began to thin. The tall, white buildings that seemed to line each street slowly melted into one continuous wall of white. When our car stopped for the last time, the driver got out in front of what appeared to be a three-story country house.

Luke turned to me and gestured toward his home, "This is Laroche Château. Jorge will show you to your quarters." He hopped out of the car and walked up the path toward the house. I watched as the front door opened as if by his will, and a tall, older man walked toward him. He greeted him warmly then immediately turned his attention toward the car. His eyes searched for me and found me still in the back seat. I squirmed nervously and noticed the driver had opened my car door and was waiting for me to exit. As I made my way to the back to grab my luggage, I was surprised to see that the tall man was already there. I'm still not sure how he closed the distance so quickly.

I forced a smile. *"Bonjour. Parlez-vous anglais?"* I asked through clenched teeth.

"Oui," he answered, but continued to speak in French, gesturing with his hands. He led me to a small, winding path that ran down the side of the house. I followed behind while I drank in my surroundings. The path ahead ran down the side of the house to what appeared to be an apartment in the back, but when my eyes ran across their lawn on the right, I was flabbergasted. I stopped, dropped my luggage and took a couple of steps in that direction. I could hear the tall man call my name, but I was in a trance. My feet began to move in that direction until I was standing at the edge of the property with a bird's-eye view of Paris.

"Paris," I whispered. Their home was sitting on the edge of a cliff, looking over the city. I wasn't aware there were any high points around Paris, so I was stunned. I searched as far as I could see to my left, then slowly let my eyes travel to the right, until they landed on the Eiffel Tower. For whatever reason, I felt tears in my eyes. The Eiffel Tower was something I'd seen pictures of my whole life, and there it was sitting right in front of me. My hands rested on a four-foot iron fence in front of me, which was the only thing standing between me and the drop. I continued to stare and was stunned when he snapped his fingers in front of my face.

"Come now," Jorge said. I looked back at the Eiffel Tower one last time, then followed.

"Laroche Château was once the home of Charles and Julia Laroche. Upon their death, it was passed down to their daughter, Eliana Laroche, Luke's late wife. Eliana's family was known around Paris for producing generations of famous artists."

"Both Luke and his wife were artists. How interesting," I commented.

Jorge studied me for a moment before turning back to the path. I heard water before seeing its source. The beautiful fountain seemed to call to me, just as clear as a mother calling her child. I happily obeyed and walked towards it. As I closed the distance, I began to hum a song I'd never heard before. Or maybe I had heard it in the airport. But it made me happy. I found my way over to an iron chair, pulled my sketchpad from my backpack, and began to draw. The sound of water filled my ears as I continued to hum the song in my head, lost in the trance of creating with no concept of time.

At some point, the tall man tried to say something, but I shooed him away and didn't let him break my peace. When my pencil stopped, the picture was complete. I looked down to appreciate what I had created and noticed a shadow move across my drawing. A cold chill ran up my spine as an eerie feeling turned inside my stomach. Searching for its origin, I looked straight into the Jorge's face. He walked in front of me, leaned over, and whispered, "Welcome home. Let me show you to your quarters."

I stood, nodded in response, and watched a warm smile spread across his face.

Chapter 13

The Plan

Christine's heels clipped along the narrow, cobbled lane. Dodging a delivery boy speeding by on a bicycle, she turned into the alley behind a café. The tall buildings that lined each side made her steps echo. She smiled and nodded to the sounds bouncing around her. She secretly loved this part of her walk home the best; the echoes sounded like many people walking together. It gave her the comfort she needed before speaking to Renae.

Arriving at the red door, she stopped and dug her keys from her purse. Knowing the door made a loud creak at the halfway point, she pushed it open slowly and shimmied inside. It was still early, at least for artists, and evidently for their agents, too. She paused at the foyer table, flipping through the pile of mail that had accumulated in her absence. She was the only one who sifted through the correspondence, so she gathered the pile and carried it into the kitchen.

"*Bonjour,*" came the voice from the small bistro table placed perfectly beside the only window in the flat with a view.

Christine groaned inwardly, then quickly closed the

distance. "*Bonjour,*" she muttered while placing a peck on each of Renae's cheeks before she could take another sip of cappuccino. "I've got news," she blurted.

Renae raised her eyebrows as she sat up with interest. "Come. Sit," she ordered.

Christine's backside had barely touched the chair before she blurted out, "I think we've found your artist." She watched Renae's cappuccino cup stop in mid-air, then quickly set back onto the table.

"Are you sure?"

"Almost positive."

Renae squealed with delight. "Tell me everything."

"You did great locating the young artist. Her name is Jan. She's still raw, but she's good."

Renae's face lit up. "Then I must plan my trip to the States and go meet her."

"No need. Here's the best part. Luke called me the night after he gave his commencement address at the art college. He told me to order three plane tickets home for the following morning, even though we had return flights booked for the following week. He said he'd accidentally run into her in a little dive bar after the art college's graduation, and he'd asked her to come back to France with him. He had been shocked when she said yes and he didn't want to give her extra time to change her mind. He also told me to call ahead to alert the staff to have the cottage ready."

Renae's fist hit the table, causing her small cappuccino cup to rattle against its saucer. "She's here? In Montmartre?"

Christine jumped. After years of Renae's outbursts, she should no longer jump. Calmly, she asked, "Why are you so angry? You wanted an artist, and I brought one right to your doorstep."

"You stupid girl. It will be so much harder now that she's

here. She will never be able to paint with Luke underfoot. You know how he is when he finds something he likes. He...” She paused for a second, then continued. “Wait. He put her in the cottage?”

“Yes.”

“Then he’s sleeping with her.”

“No,” Christine answered quickly.

Renae sat forward in her chair. “No? Why? What’s she like?”

Christine pondered how to explain, knowing that each word she said would be thoroughly examined. “First of all, she’s my age or maybe younger. She’s just finished art school. Her work shows she’s still trying to find her niche, but she’s good. No, she’s amazing. Luke is definitely interested in her, but almost in a protective way, which I’ve never seen in him before. But, from what you’ve shared with me, he might have been that way with Eliana.”

Christine watched as Renae settled back into her seat and began running her finger around the edge of the glass. Christine knew better than to comment when Renae was deep in thought. She could always see it in her eyes. They appeared to be dilated while she worked things out. Slowly, Renae’s lips began to curl into a smile.

“So, she has met Jorge?” she asked.

“Yes. When I left this morning, he was trying to get her settled into the cottage. He was barking orders to her in French while she struggled to understand. I almost felt sorry for her,” Christine admitted.

“Never feel sorry for the prey,” Renae snipped as an evil grin began to spread across her face. “This isn’t at all what we had planned, but if we play this right, it might even be better. I’ll go meet with my new artist today,” she said as she brushed the crumbs from her breakfast off the table before turning her attention to the newspaper.

The electricity bouncing around the room finally became grounded as Renae began to study the business section of the paper. Christine was grateful that Renae's attention had shifted from her, but once again, she felt the familiar sting of being dismissed.

———

RENAE WAITED UNTIL SHE COULD HEAR CHRISTINE IN THE room above before taking a slow sip of her cappuccino. She held it in her mouth for a split second, enjoying the sensation on her tongue until finally swallowing.

"What am I going to do with that girl?" Renae uttered to herself, focusing on the ceiling from where she heard Christine's pacing. She had trained Christine for years, educated her and polished her until she was the perfect assistant. Still, you can only toughen up a person so much. Underneath it all, Christine was too soft for Renae's plans. She would never go through with destroying someone's life. And, in this case, it would be destroying more than one person.

Luke had done his part. He had been reaping the benefits of stardom for years now. But with this new artist, Renae needed to put a new plan into place. Too many people would know. *This is my last one. My big farewell. And I'm taking it all,* she thought, *with or without Christine.*

Chapter 14

Friendship

J orge stood outside the closed door, his hand resting on the knob. After finding Luke's bed unmade, he went in search of his friend. It didn't feel like it had been so long ago when he would automatically bring Luke's coffee to his workroom every morning, knowing he would be there. Eight years? Nine? He'd lost count. Now, day after day, he'd find Luke still in bed as the workroom door lay open.

He continued to hold the doorknob, half dreading what he'd find on the other side while praying it would be Luke painting. There was only one way to find out. He bent over and ever so slowly began to turn the handle and push the large, paneled door. Light filled the dark hallway as he waited for his eyes to adjust.

"Bonjour, Jorge," Luke called out in a voice that seemed almost unrecognizable.

As Jorge's eyesight came into focus, he honed in on Luke pulling the sheets off of furniture. His desk and many art supplies had been covered for years. Jorge couldn't believe his eyes. He steadied himself before answering, *"Bonjour, monsieur.* Are you ready for your coffee?"

Luke moved in constant motion while answering, *"Oui. Merci."* He barely got out his answer before bursting out into laughter, which was an unfamiliar sound to Jorge. The laugh grew stronger and stronger as he flipped through half-done canvases, tossing them into a pile in the middle of the floor. Jorge didn't know whether to back out quietly or try to interact. Finally, Luke pointed to the largest canvas, which had been sitting on an easel beside his desk.

"Look at this. What in the world was I thinking?" he sputtered as he took down the canvas and added it to the growing pile.

Jorge came closer, wondering if his question hanging in the air required an answer. When he opened his mouth to speak, Luke grabbed his arm and pulled him closer. "Look, my friend. Look at all these. They are absurd. Will you please destroy them for me?"

Clearing his throat, Jorge answered, "Mrs. Seize asked me years ago to destroy all your work. That's why we have an incinerator out back."

Luke seemed surprised as he ran his hand along the early morning stubble on his cheeks. "Huh. I guess she no longer thinks of me as the artist she once did. So, you've destroyed all of the others?"

"Her orders were explicit, but if I'm being truthful, I've stored my favorites away," he replied.

Luke smiled. "Thank you for being the only person who believes in the real me." He paused for only a moment as he pieced everything together. "Although Renae was the one who got me into this mess, we're now here. I must be more careful. What would happen if this art got out into the world?" Jorge cleared his throat with a huff, making Luke answer his own question. "I'd be a laughingstock."

Jorge nodded. "You could never be a laughingstock, but I'll get rid of these immediately."

Luke wrapped him in a hug. "We've been friends for a long time. You always know what's best for me." As they parted, Luke added, "If I haven't told you this lately, thank you."

Jorge nodded and walked toward the door. He didn't quite make it before Luke stopped him with a question.

"Jorge, how's our house guest settling in?"

Although not surprised by the question, Jorge thought Luke would have waited until he had his coffee in hand. "She loved the studio. I pulled her things inside as she looked around and she seemed very happy. I believe she said something along the lines of, 'Oh man. This is really cool.'"

Luke smiled as he rearranged his paint brushes. "She's young, I know. But she's incredibly talented and sassy as hell."

"Oh, I've seen her talents. I confess, I was a little curt with her at first. But as I escorted her to the studio, she got distracted. She plopped down beside the fountain and began to sketch. Something had taken over her and she completely gave in to it. I was perturbed at first and almost reprimanded her for wasting my time, but I bit my lip and watched. What she created in those ten minutes, others would work a lifetime on. I've only seen that one other time, and that was with..." His voice trailed off to silence.

Luke stopped, with a brush in each hand. He remembered the expression on Jan's face when he found her drawing on the napkin at the bar in Savannah. He had watched for several minutes, waiting to be acknowledged. She hadn't felt his presence until she had finished her sketch. He had only seen that one other time, too. "Jorge, who was the other artist?" he asked, then held his breath, anticipating the answer.

Jorge paused. He didn't want to upset his friend, but he had to be honest. This young lady could knock Luke for a loop. He had finally come to terms with Eliana's death and had forgiven her, in his own way. This young lady was sure to dredge up feelings he had finally buried. Still, he knew Luke was just a shell of the man he once had been. The success that came with the lie of claiming another's painting wasn't really success at all. It most certainly didn't bring him happiness. The way Luke was acting this morning was living proof that he could still be happy. He looked his friend in the eye and said, "Eliana. She reminds me of Eliana. My gut tells me to protect you from her. However, we can't keep others away from us out of fear. So, I'll say only this. Be careful and know your boundaries."

Luke felt as if he had been punched in the gut and leaned over towards the pain in his stomach. He knew Jorge's statement was true. Jorge always spoke frankly with him. Luke stood up tall. "I hear you, my friend. Thank you for your concern. I'll be careful; I promise."

Jorge nodded and walked toward the door. As he pulled it shut, he heard Luke humming. He stopped to listen, remembering how Luke had always hummed when he was happy. He couldn't remember the last time he'd heard him make a joyful sound.

The thought of Luke humming made him think about Jan drawing by the fountain. She had appeared to be lost in her art, almost as if she had slipped into a different realm than the rest of the world. He had seen Eliana paint like that many times. That was definitely one of the similarities between the two artists. But the one thing that had bothered him even more was the song she was humming while she painted—*À La Claire Fontaine*. Eliana hummed the same children's lullaby when she was lost in thought. What were the odds that both women would hum the same song while painting?

His thoughts jumped back to Luke's mood this morning. Maybe, just maybe, this young lady could help him find happiness again, with or without a paintbrush in hand. Fate may have dealt Luke another hand. Only time would tell. For now, it all depended on the young woman.

Chapter 15

The Rain

I felt someone sit on the edge of my bed. *It's just Viv*, I thought, remembering how my sister would crawl into bed with me each morning when we shared the flat in Soho. I raised my eyebrows, hoping my eyes would follow in the same direction while my brain slowly put the pieces together. I was not in New York, I was in Paris, and I wasn't alone.

I jumped out of bed and spun around to find an empty bed. I knew what I felt; there was no denying it. *What is going on? Is someone in the studio with me?* I walked to the door to make sure it was locked, but as I reached for the handle, a loud knock came through. Jumping back from the door, I looked down at the flip lock. I was safe inside. Or was I? I looked around the empty room one more time. No one else was inside. The person on the other side of the door cleared their throat. I was relieved there was an actual human person. Still, I stood frozen until I heard their footsteps walking away.

I slowly cracked the door to find a tray with coffee and pastries sitting on a small, iron bistro table. After I scanned the terrace for visitors, I snuck out to retrieve the tray. But as I looked past the table, I remembered the fountain that had captured my imagination the day before. It was too beautiful out to slink back inside. I quickly glanced down at what I was wearing—a loose-fitting tank and gym shorts. Nothing was exposed. The fragrant coffee tickled my nose, inviting me to taste it. So, I slid into the chair and poured myself a cup.

"Mmmm," I hummed in appreciation. Pulling the pillow behind my back, I relaxed as I sipped the rest of the black liquid gold. My mind wandered as the fountain's water pings exploded into the awaited pond, imitating my favorite sound in the world: rain.

I always did my best work in the rain. One of my professors once told me that the rain cleansed my mind of all distractions so that my creativity could work alone. I closed my eyes and mumbled, "The rain cleanses my mind. The rain cleanses my mind. If my mind was cleansed, it would be free. Free from what? Or, free to do what?" A small smile turned up the corner of my lips. "Hmm. That's something to think about. I have no school. No job that I need to complete. No meetings. No boyfriend. No obligations. I am free. And the first thing I'm going to do is what?"

The sweet and buttery smell of the toasted croissant reached me. I grabbed it with gusto and took the largest bite of my life. Chocolate oozed out of the corners of my mouth as I rushed to pour another cup of coffee to wash it down. A small flutter of excitement hit me. *I'm in Paris and I'm totally living in the moment.*

That moment was soon interrupted by the sound of raised voices. I tried to tune them out. Whatever went on in this house was none of my business. I didn't want to intrude. But I recognized Jorge's voice. He was speaking loudly. I struggled to hear another voice, but I couldn't make out anything other than that it was female. I began to walk in that direction. My French is awful, not to mention she was speaking quickly. Angrily. His voice grew louder and louder, and so did his female counterpart. Turning my head to the side, I could hear her yelling in French with high-pitched vowel sounds.

That's when Jorge's voice changed. "*Non!*" he called out. His voice changed from anger to what? Fear? "*Non!*" he cried out again, then there was silence.

My slow walk down the covered walkway turned into a run. As I turned the corner, I saw the bumper of a black car screeching around the building and out of sight. Then immediately, I noticed Jorge lying on the ground. As I ran toward him, a large dog appeared out of nowhere, growling protectively over Jorge. I tried to get closer, but the dog's teeth were exposed as he snapped in my direction.

I stopped dead in my tracks, my heart about to jump out of my chest. The dog's vicious bark kept me at bay. I couldn't get near him. Every time I took a step toward Jorge, the animal would show his teeth and what he intended to do with them. So, I stood in place and called for help.

"Help!" I yelled. "Help. Please!" I looked past the animal and noticed Jorge wasn't moving. *Is he dead?* I focused on his chest and saw it rising and falling, but he remained still. I had to get help. I looked toward the back of the house and noticed we were near their trash area. The door next to it was left ajar, so I slowly backed away from the dog and ran inside the door.

"Hello? Anyone? Help, please!"

A young girl peeked around the corner into the kitchen. She held up her hands in question as she shook her head. "*Français?*"

"Dammit!" I yelled. I motioned for her to follow me. "Come. Please." She slowly followed. I turned and ran back out the door. Once she met me, I pointed to Jorge. Screams poured from her mouth as she ran to a panel right inside the door and pushed a button. An alarm blared through the house and into the streets.

I nodded to the girl, then turned back to Jorge and the delirious barking dog. The girl ran into the yard. As soon as the dog noticed her, he stopped barking and began to whimper. He paced around Jorge as the girl spoke to him in a calm voice.

I stayed one step behind her. She knelt beside Jorge and placed her hand over his mouth. Turning to me, she smiled and nodded, letting me know he was still breathing. I knelt beside her, so grateful that someone other than me was now taking control of the situation.

When I looked up, Luke had joined us on Jorge's other side, followed by Christine. The dog lay beside Luke and began to whine. Luke questioned the girl in French, but she was crying too hard to be understood.

This continued for what seemed like hours but was only a matter of minutes before an ambulance arrived. While the paramedics were busy securing Jorge to a gurney, a warm hand wrapped around my shoulder. I looked up to Luke's kind face.

"Are you okay, Jan?" he asked in a soft voice.

I nodded curtly as my eyes stung with tears. I fought the urge to cry. I barely knew Jorge. Still, he had been kind to me. I only wish I had arrived at his altercation a minute earlier.

"The police have some questions for you," Luke added.

I nodded once more as he extended his hand to help me to my feet. I reached out to him. When the warmth of his hand covered mine, it gave me strength and purpose. I was the only one who had witnessed Jorge's last few moments before someone left him for dead. I had to help them find out who did this.

———

Luke snuck up to his studio. The police had asked for everyone to assemble in the kitchen, but he needed a moment to calm his nerves. He stepped into his studio and locked the door behind him. No one would notice the door was shut; it had been closed for years now. Funny how just that morning he had left it open for the first time. But that time had passed quickly, and he was retreating back into the shadows.

Walking into the bathroom, he splashed water on his face. What would he do without Jorge? It had been the two of them against the world for so long. Jorge was the only one who knew about his paintings, the only one who calmed him when he struggled. What would he do if Jorge didn't make it? And what would he do while they waited to find out if he would?

"You selfish prick. Jorge is fighting for his life and you're worried about yourself," he murmured.

His thoughts went to Jan. She wasn't like everyone else around him. She spoke to him like he was a normal human being. She was the only person other than Jorge who treated him like he was just another guy.

Can I trust her? he wondered, then shook his head while answering his own question. *Not yet, but hopefully one day. Until then, I'll have to get to know her better.*

Chapter 16

Forbidden

The whole house was abuzz for the rest of the day, but I spent most of the morning in the kitchen. The young lady who had helped me, whose name I now knew was Liz, kept coffee brewing and pastries on a glass-domed platter set on the large farmhouse-style table. The police soon joined me.

"How long have you lived here? What is it you do in this household? What's your relationship with Mr. Dupris?" The first three questions were easy to answer. Then, they turned accusational. "Isn't it interesting that you were the only witness? Do you find it odd that the one person who heard the dispute didn't speak any French to tell us what was said?" Then, the final one. "What are your grievances with Jorge?"

Luke had been sitting beside me, translating anything I didn't understand and listening as I answered each question. But after the last question, he jumped to his feet. "This is the young lady's first morning in Paris. She only met Jorge yesterday. There are no grievances. We are done here. Please keep me informed if you hear anything. Thank you!"

The three officers stood, nodded curtly, and walked toward the kitchen door. The younger officer turned back to the table and grabbed a pastry before being reprimanded by his superior. The younger one winked at me and nodded, then followed his partner out.

Within the hour, I met various employees, neighbors, and finally, Luke's agent, Renae. Everyone had been very interested and asked many questions, but Renae's questions were not about Jorge. They were about me, and they were very personal. "I'd like to view your work. Are you as good as they say?"

"As good as who says?" I answered.

She snickered. "What do you hope to accomplish by forging a friendship with Luke?"

"I really wouldn't call it a friendship yet," I replied as she watched my every move.

"Then what would make you cross the Atlantic to get to us? Are you sleeping together?"

My head whipped around to lash out until I saw the look in her eyes. She was baiting me, and I wasn't going to give her the satisfaction of getting a rise out of me. I smiled before answering. "No," I said in a flat tone. She turned away from me. That's when I added, "Not yet."

She seemed surprised when I stood, and even more so when I walked around the table and sat right beside her. This time, I asked the questions. "So, Renae, are you an artist?"

"I once was."

"Were you any good?" I asked, but was met by silence. I continued. "You are Luke's agent?"

"*Oui.*"

"Have you slept with him?" I asked quickly. Again, silence.

This time, she stood. She pushed by me, walked to the counter, and placed her coffee cup into the white porcelain sink. I watched her. She was probably Luke's age, slim and put together, but there was something off. There was much more than what was seen on the surface.

Luke returned to the room and announced, "Jorge's brother is at the hospital with him. He said Jorge is stable. His head injury has caused some brain swelling. They are placing him in an induced coma until the swelling goes down."

The young maid began to cry loudly, which seemed to make Luke very uncomfortable. His eyes bounced around the kitchen, trying to find a place for them to land. Finally, he cleared his throat and said, "I must go now," and disappeared through the swinging kitchen door.

We all watched the door move back and forth until it finally stopped. I stood and nodded at Renae. "I must go, too."

Renae crossed the kitchen and held the back door open for me to leave. I stood tall and walked out. I could feel her eyes watching me from behind. I turned back just in time to watch the door slam in my face.

Thoughts of Jorge filled my mind as I followed the path back to my cottage. What could I have done differently? If I'd just been a little faster, I would have at least seen the make of the car.

Passing the bench and fountain, I noticed my breakfast tray still sitting on the table, covered in flies. With all the staff, why wouldn't someone have cleared the food? I couldn't take it back to the kitchen yet. There was no way I wanted another confrontation with Renae. I'd take it back later.

As soon as I opened the door to the cottage, I knew someone had been there. I looked over to my art supplies, open where I had left them. The first and second pencils were askew, and my sketchpad was at an odd angle. Someone had touched my art. I was so angry my hands began to shake.

Closing my eyes, I took a deep breath. I could almost picture them. Wait, not them—her. I felt her eyes on my sketches. But not Renae, different eyes. There was no hatred in them; there was concern. My eyes flew open as a cold chill ran up my spine, causing me to shiver involuntarily. The rustle of my sketches made me turn just in time to watch them float to the floor. I didn't move a muscle. Had my shiver caused them to take flight, or was it the person I envisioned when my eyes had been closed? Deep in my heart, I knew the answer.

———

My stomach growled. I had been sketching and lost track of time. Glancing out the window, I could see the colors of dusk in the sky. I hadn't eaten lunch and probably had missed dinner. *I wonder why no one has sent for me?*

My stomach rumbled again, so I decided to walk over to the house and see if someone had left me a plate. However, as I stepped through the door, I was swarmed by flies. They had been in a free-for-all smorgasbord for hours now and must have asked all their friends and families to join them. I had never seen so many greedy insects. I danced toward the fly buffet, swinging my arms back and forth and jumping up and down, trying to clear them enough to grab the tray, but they didn't go far. They buzzed nearby, waiting for my movement to stop. I decided not to give them one second, so I broke into a skip-like dance. I zigged and zagged down the path all the way to the main house and let myself in the kitchen door.

Once inside, I looked out the window at the stragglers. "Ha-ha, suckers!" I said through the glass. Suddenly aware of my temporary insanity, I glanced around the kitchen and was thankful no one had been there to witness my craziness. After clearing my breakfast tray, I was no longer hungry.

Where is everyone? I peeked my head through the kitchen door. "Hello?" I called out to an empty house. I slowly walked into a hallway that led to an elaborate dining room. I continued to walk the entire first floor until I found myself standing at the bottom of the stairs, contemplating where to go up.

"Hello?" I called again, and slowly began to ascend the stairs. Thoughts of *Beauty and the Beast* tugged from my childhood memories. "Do not set foot in the west wing," Belle was told. "What's in the west wing?" she had asked innocently, to be scolded by the answer of, "It's forbidden."

I smiled at the thought and continued upward. The stairs took a turn to the left, and I followed. My nerves had tightened the muscles in my stomach, making me feel breathless. I made myself relax and took a deep breath. There is something both exhilarating and terrifying about things that are forbidden.

The stairs emptied into a long hallway. Although it was dark paneled, it wasn't dark. Many small candelabras hung from the high ceilings at perfect intervals and were dotted by wall sconces that alternated for complete light coverage. Yet what surprised me was that every door was closed except for one.

I called out, once again, "Hello. Is anyone here?" but was met by silence. I decided to just peek my head into the open door. I wouldn't walk inside. Except that when I got to the doorway, I realized it was Luke's studio.

I knew better. I had just gotten mad that someone was in my space earlier. But that was different; they touched my stuff. *I'll just have a quick look.* My mom's voice entered my head. "Eyes only. Do not touch, Jan."

Easels sat empty around the room, but there were a couple of canvases in a pile in the middle of the floor as if waiting to be thrown away. *I'll just walk in and see what he is going to dispose of.* Squatting down, I picked up the first one. *Wait. I'm confused. This doesn't look like his work.* I picked up the second and knew it must belong to someone else. *Who is painting in here?*

I was interrupted by the sound of a woman clearing her throat. I had been so deep in thought that I hadn't heard her enter the room. I turned into the smiling face of a woman I remembered seeing earlier in the kitchen.

"Can I help you find your way?" she asked.

"Yes. *Oui.* I'm lost," I answered. I felt the blush rise into my cheeks. *Yeah, right. I'm lost all the way up to the second floor.* She seemed to believe me, though, and laughed at my supposed stupidity.

"Come. Follow me," she replied.

I followed her down to the front door. She was older, but mousey, and seemed to be sweet. She directed me to the path that led back to the cottage. I thanked her dutifully and walked off in the direction given. It wasn't until I passed the fountain that I felt my stomach rumble in hunger. It was going to be a long night.

I pulled out the schedule Christine gave me when I arrived and noticed the next thing on it wasn't until Tuesday at ten. Luke was going to be interviewed at his gallery for an international art show. Smiling, I thought about how I had the next day all to myself. *I can't wait to get lost in Montmartre.*

Chapter 17

Gerard's Neighborhood

From the minute my feet hit the ground, I knew I had to get out on the streets. All I wanted to do was sketch. I pulled on a pair of jeans, threw my hair up in a pony-tail, tossed my supplies in my extra-large tote, and bolted out the door. I had barely taken two steps before running into Luke.

"*Bonjour.* Where are you running off to this morning?"

I didn't want to sound like an obsessed, crazy person, but if the shoe fits, wear it. "I have no plan, but I woke up and just had to create." My eyes searched for something to focus on. Admitting that I was not in control of my actions was scary. Finally, my eyes met his. He was grinning from ear to ear.

"I recognize that look in your eye. It's been a while, but I remember it. I could never be the one who stands between your passion and your canvas. We'll talk later."

"Any word on Jorge?" I asked.

"Everything's the same. No news seems to be good news." He looked away, but I could see the worry on his face.

"Do you need me to..."

He put his finger to his lips. "Go," he said in a whisper, shooing me away, then turning back toward the house.

Not many people understand the creative process or the desire to create. He did, and he respected it. I made my way to the street where I had seen the car depart from the back of the house, then followed the sidewalk that ran beside it. The road had plenty of twists and turns and went in many directions. I walked for the better part of an hour, mentally marking spots I wanted to come back and draw while devouring pastries from every bakery I passed. I was almost at the point of heading back when I was walking down what I thought was a dead-end alley. But once I got to the end, it opened up to the exact spot I'd been looking for.

Tears sprang to my eyes. I had almost doubted the place existed, but here I stood. Closing my eyes, I listened for him. Was the boyhood spirit of my grandfather still here, running the streets and getting into trouble? He wouldn't have known at that time that he would move to a foreign country. I listened harder but became distracted by the toasty smell of coffee. My nose led me to a very small bistro with only four two-seater tables in front. I snagged the only one that was unoccupied, ordered café créme and pain au chocolat, and pulled out my sketchpad.

I sketched all day. My breakfast turned into lunch. When the family said they were closing to take their lunch, they allowed me to stay. I was still sketching when they returned for the dinner crowd. I couldn't pull myself away. It became even more beautiful when the yellow-amber from the streetlights began to glow. I sketched it four different times, each angle focusing on something different, each adding different colors. Then, I added the people whom I imagined would have been there at that time. The children in the streets. The shopkeepers. People living their daily lives.

When I finally stood to begin packing my things, I had a group of people surrounding me. The bistro owner asked if they could look at my sketches, so I spread all of them across the table. The locals smiled, pointing out particular items from each sketch. I noticed an elderly lady in the back. She seemed extra curious. She waited her turn, then approached the table. She studied each drawing, then turned her focus to me. I nodded and began to smile, but then noticed the tears building in her eyes. They spilled over quickly and ran down her face. She didn't wipe them away; her focus was completely on me. She asked me a question in French.

I replied, "*Non parlez français.*"

She nodded and spoke in her best English. "Who are you? How do you know such things?"

"I'm just an artist," I answered.

"This was my life many years ago," she whispered as she pointed to a little girl in the picture. "This is me. My mother gave me this blue coat for my birthday. I fell down and it ripped this very day, the day the man had this monkey in the square." She reached out and took my hand.

I didn't know how to explain that I could picture it in my mind. I didn't want her to think I was something I wasn't. Finally, I answered. "My grandfather grew up here. He was an artist, too. He painted this spot before he passed away. I've been searching for it."

"Who was your grandfather?"

"Gerard Laroche. And my name is Janine," I answered.

The color seemed to drain from her face. She took in a deep breath as she closed her eyes. Another tear slid down her cheek before she opened them. "I always wondered if he made it out safely. He was my husband's cousin. Their fathers were brothers."

"Then I'm related to your husband?" I asked, already knowing the answer but trying to make sense of it all.

"*Oui*. You are related. My name is Anne." She squeezed my hand a little tighter before letting go. "I must get home now. My husband is waiting. Are you staying in Montmartre?"

"Yes."

"Will you come visit me, please?"

"Yes. I'd love to."

She pointed to a flat across the street. "Mornings are best. My husband is ill, so he gets tired in the afternoons. I only snuck out tonight for our favorite dessert, madeleines.

"I understand." We smiled at each other, both of us lost in another time. "I'll be back, Anne. I look forward to our meeting."

She turned to walk away but stopped. She placed her hand on mine and whispered, "There was once another like you. Be careful who you share your art with. And stay away from Luke Dupris. I don't want you to meet the same fate as Eliana." She patted my hand and walked toward her flat.

What was that? The same fate as Eliana? Are you kidding me? I shivered involuntarily, still watching as Anne reached her doorway. She looked back at me and tilted her head. The intensity of her eyes showed me she knew. She raised her hand before walking inside and closed the door behind her.

Chapter 18

Control

I soon got into a daily routine of discovering Montmartre, uncovering its secrets at every turn. I would explore with a sketchbook in hand, pausing when something called to me. Since the day I found my grandfather's boyhood neighborhood, I was able to see things differently. I could envision how places looked in the past. Sometimes it was when they were built. Sometimes, it was during the war. Each one felt different and seemed to tell me how it desired to be seen.

Each day, I fell further in love with this intimate section of Paris, known for its ability to soothe an artist's soul. Walking the same streets where Pablo Picasso, Pierre-Auguste Renoir, Claude Monet, Vincent van Gogh, and Henri Matisse had lived gave me a perspective on my life as an artist that I had not grasped before. I had been in such a hurry to sketch and sell my work, that I had lost my purpose. I had been creating for others instead of creating because I had the ability to do so.

I began to see Luke every afternoon. Some nights, he would be waiting for me by the fountain when I arrived home. He was always curious, but cautious. He'd always ask the same question. "Where did you adventure off to today?" And I'd always answer the same. "Come in, and I'll show you."

He seemed to get a kick out of the scenes I chose to sketch, things that he walked by every day and never found art worthy. Now, they were set back in time and appeared differently. The man stacking his fresh baguettes in a cart. The sprig of lavender growing out of a large clay pot with the windmill as a backdrop. Barrels lined up on a small, cobbled walkway. The line of artists painting silhouettes in the square, or the hundreds of steps leading up to Paris' highest point at Sacre Coeur. He studied each one and always left me with a comment, sometimes not a good one.

It wasn't until the night he saw the painting of my grandfather's boyhood home that he was speechless. I had sketched it days before but had spent the last two nights painting from my sketch. I had accidentally left it on an easel in the corner, and Luke had seen it as soon as he walked in the door.

I watched his eyes move slowly over the canvas, inspecting every inch. I felt exposed, like I was being undressed. I was embarrassed by my nakedness and wanted to hide. He turned to me with passion in his eyes. My painting moved him, physically and emotionally. I'd never experienced anything like this before. He was speechless. The tables had turned. I no longer needed his feedback or approval. Our eyes met and neither of us turned away.

"What now?" he asked, his voice hoarse and barely audible.

I was in control of whatever came next. What did I want? Boldly, I answered, "I'm going to take a long, hot shower and get dressed. I'll be ready at 8:30 for you to take me to dinner."

His eyes searched mine before answering, "I can hardly wait." He leaned in, kissing both my cheeks softly. Slowly. He hovered for the smallest second above my lips before pulling back. The look of confusion on his face surprised me. He was battling with something, but what, I had no idea. His eyes went to my lips, then slowly back to my eyes. "Until then," he added, then turned and left.

The restaurant was something straight out of a dream. We descended a winding path by the glow of streetlights, which were mounted on each side of the building walls. The path grew narrower and the electric streetlights changed to candles. When we reached the restaurant, the doorway and front windows were propped open and soft music spilled out onto the street.

Luke reached for my hand as we approached, then escorted me inside. The cozy room sat only five tables, four of which were occupied. However, the table in the back nook sat open. Luke didn't wait for the host but walked straight to the table. Every patron turned toward him.

"*Bonsoir*, Luke," they called out. He nodded as he moved along, only stopping once to greet an older woman, kissing her on each cheek before moving past.

He ushered me to our table, where he held my chair. Once seated, he asked my permission to remove the taupe wrap I had draped around my shoulder. He unwrapped me like a precious gift, slowly, letting his fingers move across my shoulder. I shivered in response. He pulled his chair closer to mine and poured from the bottle of wine that was magically waiting for us.

Glancing around at the intimate setting, I said, "This is incredible."

"Thank you," he answered.

He must have noticed my confusion and began to explain. "I own it. Well, actually, I'm the investor in a very talented chef."

As if on cue, the chef turned the corner. He also greeted Luke with a double kiss, then turned his attention to me. A smile spread across his face as he moved in closer. I held out my hand to shake his, but he quickly bypassed it as he leaned in further.

"Oh, hey. So, we're going in for a kiss? Okay," I mumbled as he planted a loud double on me, too.

"I'm so pleased to have you dine with us tonight, *mona mi*. It's very nice to meet you. I'm Victor." He then turned to Luke with a knowing smile and went back to the kitchen.

Luke held up his glass to mine. "*Santé*," he said as we chimed in unison.

"*Santé*," I responded. Taking a sip of the sweet beverage, I closed my eyes, letting the warm liquid make its way down. When I opened them, Luke was watching me. Nervously, I filled the silence. "The chef seems nice. You must eat here often."

"Yes, we are great friends and I do eat here often, but always alone. That's why he greeted you so warmly; he's happy I'm not alone tonight. He always feels obliged to sit with me."

I only nodded. Was this man as alone as he seemed to be? I took another sip of wine, then asked, "Why are you always alone?"

"As you know, I'm a widower. And sadly, we were never able to have children together. So, obviously, that leaves me alone," he answered.

"Yes. But that is by choice. You're a celebrity, you're nice looking, and you could have any woman you want. Why are you not dating?"

"I could have any woman?" he asked.

I felt the heat rise up my neck to my face. I calmed myself. "Why aren't you dating?" I asked once again.

He shrugged and began to say something when our conversation was interrupted by the waiter bringing the first course. The French onion soup was followed by a classic green salad, then a zucchini pasta dish, savory beef stew, salmon with small, purple potatoes, and then, when I thought we were done, the waiter brought us sticky toffee pudding and coffee. Our conversation had been light throughout the meal, but as the coffee was poured, I felt a shift.

I began, "Luke, why have you been alone for so long?"

He leaned in ever so slightly. Paused, as if trying to find the right words, then blurted out, "I'm being haunted."

His eyes fell from mine as his gaze moved to the floor. He ran his hand through his hair before turning his attention back to me. I saw the sadness and the worry, but most of all, I saw the fear. Then, in a quiet whisper, he continued, "I'm being haunted by my dead wife."

———

As I lay in bed, I replayed the events of the evening. Of course, our date was over the second that conversation began. Was it a date at all? I'll probably never know, and I'm fine with that. Really, I didn't need a grieving older man with issues in my life right now. And boy, he sure had issues. That wasn't a normal romantic dinner conversation. I sighed. Something I only did when I was worried. Maybe his confession was upsetting me more than I want to admit. Or maybe I was upset for prying into his life. I couldn't help that I was interested. Probably more than I wanted to admit. I'd have to apologize to him tomorrow after his big interview.

Turning on my side, I looked out the window. The wind had picked up, and the clematis vine, which was planted around the window, began to sway. It cast a moving shadow on the bed with my white quilt being its movie screen. I watched it jump and dance around until my eyes became heavy. I smiled with a childhood feeling of peace passing over me. *Tonight may have ended strangely, but I'm in Paris and I'm painting like I never have before.* I took a long blink. My thoughts morphed over to Luke's wife. She'd walked these same streets, sat at the fountain outside, and slept in this very bed. We were somehow joined, at least by our love of art. My eyes became heavier as my blinks became longer. As I finally closed my eyes for the night, my last thoughts were of her. I could picture her showing me her work. She seemed happy, almost proud. But as my view spun to observe her painting, I realized it wasn't her painting at all; it was her husband's most famous masterpiece, "Ascend." I glanced back at her in confusion. She was shaking her head at me, and that's when I knew—I was being haunted, too.

Chapter 19

Calling Home

Savannah, Georgia

Agnes glanced at the clock. 5:35 a.m. She wasn't running too far behind. She didn't open until seven. She hurriedly shoved the last tray of cinnamon rolls into the oven and set the timer. She was startled when the phone rang. *No one ever calls before six,* she thought as she hastily wiped her hands on a rag and walked toward the phone.

"Aggie's Café," she answered, half holding her breath until she found out who the caller was.

"Agnes, I was hoping you'd be in the shop already," Jan blurted out. "I questioned the time difference but really wanted to talk with you, so I went ahead and called."

"Jan. Oh my gosh. How are you? How's Paris?"

"It's beautiful. So, so beautiful."

"And how's the famous Luke Dupris?"

"He's very nice, and surprisingly, very normal."

"And sexy?"

"Well, of course. But it's not like that. Listen, I've got a favor to ask. I'd like you to sell my art."

"Uh, I already sell your art."

"Yes. I know. But I've had, let's just say, a revelation. Could you sell it all? I want to get rid of anything I've painted in the past. I wasn't painting from the soul. You can keep whatever you want for the café and sell the rest."

"Wow, Jan. Are you sure? Have you put enough thought into this?"

"I'm positive. But is this too much to ask of you?"

"Of course not. I'll get the tribe to help me get everything out of your apartment and I'll have them hanging by the week's end."

"Perfect. How is everyone?"

Agnes laughed. "You know us. There's always an adventure happening. But none of them are the same without you. We sure do miss you."

"Man, I miss y'all too. Give everyone my love. And thanks again for handling this. Gotta run. Much love!"

The line went dead just as Agnes was saying, "Bye. Have fun." She hung up the phone and thought about what Jan had just said. How could she want to sell all of her art after two weeks of being in Paris? What kind of revelation was she talking about?

The sound of the timer going off interrupted her thoughts. There was never time to be distracted during her workday. She'd have to unravel all this when she met her friends for lunch the following day.

"I THOUGHT I'D BE THE LAST ONE HERE," MAGGIE announced as she scooted up her upholstered chair under the white clothed table at The Chart House. Nodding toward the empty seat, she said, "At least I beat Jan."

"I totally blanked when I made the reservation," Stephanie replied. "I guess that's what happens when people disappear into the night without saying goodbye."

"In her defense, she did leave me a message, in the middle of the night, saying that she had been given a great opportunity to go to Paris and would be leaving early the next morning. She also asked me to send her love to the tribe. So, she did inform us —just not in person," Kathleen replied.

"Who does that?" Latrice snips. "Who just up and leaves for Paris in the span of twelve hours?"

Stephanie snickered. "You do, Latrice. Remember telling us that story of you and that guy hopping on a train after class and going to Paris without any luggage or anything? What was his name?"

Latrice squirmed before answering. "Nicholas. His name was Nicholas. And yes, I definitely do remember, but that was different," Latrice rebuked. "We were in London and still in college. We all did dumb shit in college. But we're not young and dumb anymore. Besides, Jan still beats herself up about running off to New York after high school. Remember when she came back? She told us she'd never do anything dumb like that again. And...here we are."

"It's been two weeks. Has anyone got a postcard from her?" Maggie asked. The table all shook their heads. "Good. I was worried I was the only one who hadn't."

The horn from a passing ship drew everyone's attention down to the river. It gave Agnes the opportunity she needed to tell them the news. "Jan called me yesterday morning."

All heads turned to Agnes, but Kathleen was the first one to speak. "What's wrong?" she blurted out. Kathleen's Irish roots always made her believe that disaster was right around the corner.

"Nothing's wrong. At least, that's what she said. But get

this. She asked me to get y'all to help me get all her art from her apartment and sell it at the café. Oh, and she said to send you her love."

"That's weird. She's been painting for months, trying to get enough pieces for an art show," Stephanie added.

"She said she had a revelation and she's painting clearer now, whatever that means," Agnes explained.

The table was quiet, each one processing what they had been told until Latrice couldn't hold it in any longer. "That's the craziest shit I've heard all day. And I work in government, so believe me, I've heard some crazy shit. Are we really gonna do this?"

The table turned to Agnes. "I told her we would. She was not confused. In fact, she sounded more confident than she ever has before."

After lunch, the tribe exited the building onto Factors Walk. They each meandered around, not wanting to leave one another so quickly. They stood along the iron rail, looking over the Barnard Street ramp, watching the people walk along River Street below. A tugboat slowly made its way down the river while the sound of a lone saxophone played a soft Southern tune.

"I know Jan must be having fun in France. But look at our beautiful city. It doesn't get any better than this," Stephanie said.

"Yes, it could, if we all didn't have to go back to work," Latrice answered. "But here we are, six bad-ass females making our mark on our fair city."

"Five," Kathleen corrected. "Speaking of the sixth, let's figure out a night to go get Jan's art."

They all agreed to meet Sunday night. The job was easy; Jan had her paintings stacked against a wall in her apartment, almost as if she knew they were coming for them.

After they moved all the paintings into the café, Agnes made them appetizers. She set them on the middle table along with a bottle of wine and five coffee mugs. "Sorry about the glasses. But this is a café. These are my finest mugs."

They admired Jan's art as they munched on fried green tomato BLT bites, cold chicken curry skewers, and cinnamon rolls Agnes had hidden away from the morning crowd.

"She really is a talented artist, isn't she?" Stephanie commented.

"Yes, she is. And if she's ready to sell all these, I can't imagine what the new lot looks like," Kathleen responded, "Let's keep her in our thoughts and prayers. We all know how hard self-revelations can be."

"Yep. We sure do," Agnes added.

"Cheers to Jan," Maggie announced.

"Cheers to Jan!" they all replied as the clunky coffee mugs of wine all clattered together.

Chapter 20

The Tuesday Interview

Montmartre, France

I'd never been good at following advice, but as I approached Luke's gallery, I could hear Anne's voice just as clear as if she were standing beside me.

I thought I would arrive early and help with all the last-minute things that inevitably fall apart right before a showing. Thirty minutes before a show in France is much different than thirty minutes before a show in Savannah. I should have known better; he is world-renowned. But somehow over the last couple of days, he'd become just another artist friend to me, so I was surprised by the line to get inside.

The string of people blocked the small street, which was lined with stores. Locals and tourists pushed through to get inside a bakery, bookstore, and gift shop. People were coming and going inside each shop, while the line of people maneuvered, keeping their places. *This is crazy*, I thought. *These store owners must hate being so close to all this activity.* Yet, it seemed to work. There was an excitement in the air; I felt the buzz. Somehow, the wait had heightened the anticipation to get inside.

Step by step, I drew closer. Until finally, I was able to look inside the front window. Luke looked nervous. He was pacing the floor, flipping through notecards, oblivious to everyone around him. *I wonder if he's always like this.* I'd seen many of his interviews over the years, and he always appeared to be so calm and sure of himself. The thought of our conversation ran through my mind. I was still unsure of why he admitted that he felt he was being haunted so freely to me. Something about his vulnerability made me anxious to get inside and try to help him in some way.

When I got to the doorway, Renae and a portly young man were going through names on a list, snickering as they spoke to one another in hushed voices. She was dressed elegantly in a black pantsuit that showed all her curves, topped off with a red cashmere shawl, draped dramatically across her shoulders. She scanned the names, pretending not to know me, then rolled her eyes and checked me off. She thrust a pamphlet in my hand before turning to the person in line behind me.

The first face I recognized inside was Christine's. She was trying to manage the crowd and encouraging people to move inside a display room in the back, where chairs were set for the interview. As I walked in her direction to offer my help, I noticed the crowd around me had stopped moving and was staring at me, or so I thought. I felt someone touch my elbow, and I turned right into Luke's chest. Our collision made him laugh. It was a welcoming sound, so different from the Luke I had watched pacing through the window.

"Can you help me with something?" he whispered in my ear. I nodded. "Come with me."

I followed him through the crowd. Everyone cleared a path for him as he walked. When we reached the front of the room, I noticed a small stage-like area with two chairs set up facing one another. We walked into a small room off to its side and he closed the door.

"I thought I could do this alone, but I can't. Jorge has always been there to help with television interviews. I never have a problem talking about my work to crowds, but when I know it's being televised, I ramble. Jorge and I came up with a system." He handed me the index cards he had been studying. "These are my talking points. I need to mention all five of them. I don't have a problem talking; I just need to stay on point. All you need to do is sit in a chair I have marked off and hold up your finger to the numbered card. I'll work that subject into the conversation at that time. Just make sure that once it's covered, you turn that card around."

"Your interview begins in five minutes. Can't Renae do this? She knows you best."

His cynical smirk surprised me. "No, she doesn't. You're perfect for this."

"I don't have time to study these cards beforehand," I explain.

"No need. Just look over them and hold up your finger to which one applies the most to the interviewer's question."

"What if I give you the wrong number answer?"

Luke squeezed my arm. "You won't."

I looked down at the cards and began to read. The headings were simple—What inspired this painting? How to keep a worldwide presence. We all have a responsibility to our communities. What I'm working on now. The digital world of art.

"Okay. This seems straightforward enough."

"Good girl. Follow me," he said, and led me to my seat.

Things moved quickly. The crowd was all seated, and the lights and cameras were all on. I sat on the edge of my seat.

Why in the world would he have asked me to do this? There would have to be someone better qualified for this job. I watched as the interviewer addressed the crowd and horror filled me. She spoke in French. I couldn't understand one word. The crowd laughed as she fed them lines I couldn't understand. I had forgotten all about where I was. I stood to leave, but I felt a hand on my shoulder.

"What are you doing?" Christine asked between gritted teeth. "You must remain seated. We are live."

"It's in French. The interview is in French," I stated.

"You really need to learn our language if you're planning on living here," she said softly. Then, irritated, she explained that the interview itself would be conducted in English since it would be broadcast internationally.

I exhaled loudly just as Luke walked onto the stage. He smiled at the crowd, then nodded at me. I smiled back in response. Once he was seated, the announcer turned to the camera.

"Hi, I'm Katherine Talbot. I'm coming to you live from Montmartre, France, where I have the privilege to interview Luke Dupris at Gallery Laroche. Hi, Luke."

I listened intently, holding up my fingers at the appropriate time while Luke acknowledged me with a nod that was so slight that only I noticed. He was a natural. He spoke eloquently and engaged anyone listening. As the interview came to an end, I breathed a sigh of relief. That's when Ms. Talbot added one last question.

"It is said that you have hit a dry spell. You were introducing the world to a beautiful new piece of art every year for four years straight. It has been three years since your last masterpiece. Has the pressure of painting something marvelous halted your inspiration to paint at all? Are you in a slump?"

Luke froze. He locked eyes with me. I shuffled through the

cards on my lap until I found a card I'd already used. Number I—What inspires you? He smiled slightly and ever so calmly addressed Ms. Talbot. "An artist knows no time. They are inspired daily by the simple things in life. Sometimes, it may be as small as a bee flying in the garden or as large as Sacre Coeur itself. I have many projects I'm working on, but I'm on no one's timeline but my own."

She leaned up on the edge of her seat, ready to address his comment, when Luke took control. "Thank you so much for this interview." Then, he addressed the people in the audience. "And thank you so much to the wonderful people who are with me today. You are the reason I paint. *Au revior*." He stood and walked off the stage and into the small room, closing the door behind him. The announcer was visibly angry. She hadn't been able to catch him off guard. Her eyes quickly jumped to Luke's focal point—me. I smiled, instead of ignoring her stare, and offered her an exaggerated wave.

"What are you doing?" Christine whispered through clenched teeth before grabbing my waving hand. "Stop it!"

"She's not a nice person, sitting up there smiling to the world. Now she knows that I see she's a snake," I answered.

"She doesn't care what you think. You're a pion."

Ms. Talbot rolled her eyes at me, then scanned the room. She was looking for someone. She shook her head ever so slightly at them before busying herself taking off her microphone. I quickly turned in the direction of her gaze to the back of someone walking away. There was no doubt who the person was. Renae stood out in her red cashmere shawl.

Chapter 21

The Train to Avignon

I was exhausted. My neck hurt from leaning over my canvas. My hands were sore from drawing. And my mind was foggy from all the coffee I had drunk. All I wanted to do was climb into a hot bath with a glass of wine, then slide into the cold of the white, crisp sheets on my bed. I grunted out loud when I saw the note pinned to my door: "Please come to the house when you get in. There is much to discuss."

Can I just pretend I didn't see the note? Guilt got hold of me, so I stashed away my art and walked over to the main house.

I opened the front door to a darkened house. The only light I could see came through the glass French doors of the formal office. I decided to call out, "Luke? Are you home?"

No one answered. I walked toward the office door, calling for him again, but no answer. It was strange that he would ask me to walk over but not be listening for me. I reached the door and raised my hand to knock; that's when I saw him sitting at his desk. His head was leaning back onto the chair strangely. I got a weird feeling in my gut. *Is he dead? Should I go in to find out?* I looked back into the darkened house. The front door was open. Had I left it open? The hairs on my arm raised and I shivered. I quickly turned back to the desk, but Luke wasn't there. *Where is he?* The doors of the office flew open and I screamed. Luke jumped back but then began to laugh.

"I thought you were dead," I yelled angrily.

"Dead? Good gosh. Why?"

"You looked dead, all slumped over on your desk."

He laughed again. "I don't sleep well at night, so sometimes I fall asleep in random places."

"Well, you scared me half to death. And then, I noticed I left the front door open." As I turned to close it, I realized it had already been closed. Luke didn't seem surprised; he only nodded. Obviously, this had happened to him, too.

"I got your note. What's up?" I asked.

"It's late now, but I wanted to see if you'd like to go to Avignon with me tomorrow for a few days. Provence is beautiful; I think you'd like it.

"I don't know, Luke. I'm kind of on fire right now and learning so much here. I'd hate to break my streak."

"Why would you break it? Imagine lavender fields and medieval towns. I'll try and stay out of your way. Come on."

I began to picture the rolling hills of lavender in their many shadowy shades. "Okay. I'd love to."

"Very good. The train leaves at five p.m. tomorrow."

"You already bought my ticket?"

He smiled. "Every artist wants to experience the lavender fields."

I hated when people assumed things about me. I almost told him I'd changed my mind. But I really did want to see those fields. *Damn him; he's right.* "Okay. I'll see you tomorrow." I turned to leave. When I got to the front door, I noticed it was propped open again. Maybe it would do me some good to get away from here for a couple of days.

———

THE TRAIN BOUNDED OUT OF PARIS, LEAVING THE CITY IN a blur. I was happy to see the sprawling countryside without a hill in sight. The steep streets in Montmartre had worked my calves harder than any lunge challenge had ever done in the past. It was nice to see flat land again, so much like what I was used to in Savannah.

I was excited to spend the three-hour train ride to Avignon alone with Luke. Little did I know that he would fall asleep like a toddler after five minutes bouncing on the moving train. I watched out the window as we flew through the countryside, trying my best to focus on towns and houses in the distance, wondering what the people inside were doing. Cooking. Cleaning. Raising their families. The whole country had been ravaged by wars, plagues and poverty. Generations later, they were strong and proud. My only knowledge of the French so far had been given to me in Montmartre. Still, the people I had met so far were passionate about what they did and who they belonged to. Their families, their Father, and their art.

I glanced over at Luke, happy he was asleep so I could study him well. He appeared to be in his mid-forties. No wrinkles, but a touch of grey on his temples. He was nice-looking, I guess, in a very French way. Very manicured, which was different than most men his age in Savannah who had grown up near the water. They tended to be rugged, tanned, and easy-going.

Something made his face twitch and his hand rose to wipe his forehead. I quickly looked away so as not to get caught staring and turned my focus out the window. I was happy when his breathing returned to a nice rhythm.

What's his deal? I couldn't get a grasp on him. He's a big-time artist, but when I wandered into his studio, his work was average at best. *If* that was indeed his work. It looked nothing like his famous pieces. I realize artists can change their style, but it was such a drastic change that it made me wonder if something had happened to him—either physically or emotionally.

To be fair, I knew emotionally he had the tragic death of his wife, but could that have changed his style? Then, there was the wife's haunted studio. *Should I share that with him, or could I have imagined everything?*

The train jerked. Luke sat up in his seat. I could feel him staring. He pushed a stray piece of hair from my forehead before speaking. "Did you say something?"

"No. I've just been enjoying my view." I lied. It wouldn't be the last time I would lie to him. But at least by then, I'd be in control of my emotions.

Chapter 22

The Medieval City

A car was waiting at the station when we arrived in Avignon at eight p.m.

"Avignon is a medieval city that has been modernized and stretched over time, but the original city walls, which encircle historic Avignon, still remain," Luke explained. "My flat lies inside."

I was surprised when our car dropped us in the center of the city until I noticed the streets were all sidewalk size, allowing no room for automobiles. I pulled my bag behind Luke as he snaked his way down the streets full of restaurants, shops, and grocery stores. We turned right and left so many times that the streets began to all look the same. Finally, he stopped in front of a doorway.

"Here we are," he announced as he fished the key out of his pocket and pushed open a heavy wooden door into a large square foyer. There was one door just inside, which Luke explained belonged to the caretaker, Claude. A white marble staircase began on the left and ascended the wall, then turned right until it reached the second floor.

Luke picked up his travel bag and began to climb. As if reading my mind, he called over his shoulder, "There are no lifts in Avignon."

Maybe he should have mentioned that before I packed my entire bag for this venture. Mustering all my strength, I lifted the suitcase with both hands and made it at least eight steps before setting it down. I looked up to check my progress, only to realize I was not even halfway, so I decided to pull it step-by-step.

Ba-bump. Ba-bump. Ba-bump. The sound bounced around the room. I began to laugh, which made my attempts even more awkward and louder.

"Do you need some help?" he asked.

"No, no. I've got it," I laughed.

I barely heard the caretaker come out of his apartment until he began yelling up to me from the bottom of the stairs. His angry form of the beautiful French language sounded as if something was caught in his throat.

I glanced down through the stairs' marble spindles and said, "*Bonjour,*" in my best Southern French.

This time, he began to stomp up behind me, still speaking quickly, until he turned the corner stair and saw Luke. They began to speak politely to one another as I continued to climb.

Ba-bump. Ba-bump. "One more," I yelled as the final ba-bump sounded off.

Luke clapped at my accomplishments. "Follow me," he announced as he opened a second door into a large, welcoming room. I wasn't expecting such a warm space. Dark leather sofas, which appeared to be worn soft, were the first thing I noticed. The end of the room held build-in red bookshelves full of beautifully bound novels of all sizes, with a cozy upholstered chair next to them, perfect for sitting in and reading. There was a large farmhouse table with a trough centerpiece of fresh fruit and an open kitchen with a porcelain sink and shiny, sterling appliances.

"This is your place?" I asked.

"You seem surprised."

"It's not at all like your home in Montmartre. This one is very comfortable and livable."

"The house in Montmartre belonged to Eliana's family. This house belonged to mine. I didn't have the privilege of wealth like my wife. My parents worked hard as laypeople in the Catholic Church, running the papal palace here in Avignon. I knew if I wanted to be an artist, I had to move to Paris, so I did.

"Where are your parents now?"

"They decided to move to Vatican City to be curators at the Vatican Museums. This flat has been in the family for years, and they didn't want to let go of it, so they gave it to their one and only son, me. I actually have been to it more in the last five years than in the last twenty. It's the only place I can get away from..." He paused and looked straight into my eyes.

"The only place you can get away from Eliana?" I asked.

His brow furrowed as he nodded.

I reached out to him. I'm not sure why, but I wanted to comfort him in some way. His oxford shirt sleeves were rolled up, so my hand landed on his bare forearm. The cold of his skin, in the ninety-degree heat, surprised me.

Luke slowly pulled his arm away as he cleared his throat. "You must be hungry. Claude said he left us a platter in the fridge. Have a seat," he said, motioning to the long table. He disappeared into the long kitchen and returned with a board of meats, cheese, crackers, and pears. I felt my stomach growl in response. He poured us a full glass of red wine, then straddled a barstool across from me. "*Bon appétit,*" he said softly.

I was unsure of the proper way to eat off the board, so I

waited for him to eat first. He picked up a piece of salami, folded it onto a cracker, and popped it into his mouth. I followed. We picked and ate in silence. Unlike our nice dinner together in Montmartre, he seemed to be lost in his thoughts, and I didn't dare to interrupt. As soon as I finished my glass of wine, I stood. "I'm pretty tired; I think I'll turn in early tonight."

He nodded. "The guest rooms are upstairs and each door is open. There are three to choose from."

"Thank you, Luke," I said softly. "Goodnight."

He nodded again and forced a small smile, so I turned and left the room. His lack of interest during dinner made me feel like I'd done something wrong. What would make someone flip-flop their moods so quickly? I was deep in thought until I came to the bottom of the next set of stairs. These were smaller and would take a lot more effort to climb.

I stood up tall to muster all my strength before I began my next journey, which actually turned out to be easier than the previous set of stairs. Maybe the food had given me strength, or more likely, the wine had eased the pain. Once at the top, I surveyed all the rooms and chose the front room, which faced the small street. Swinging the window open, I was able to get a full view of the street below. People were talking as they passed, unaware of my listening. Not that I could understand what they were saying.

My thoughts jumped back to Luke. Was he doubting his decision to bring me to Avignon? Or worse than that, bringing me to France at all? *I can't worry about that. I am here and whether he's happy with me or not, I'm gonna enjoy every minute of being in Provence.*

Chapter 23

The Dinner Party

I woke to the sound of voices. I had fallen asleep last night listening to the chatter on the streets and forgot to close the window. I heard the sound of people saying good morning to one another as they passed. Then, the sound of a store opening next door. I lay in bed, wondering what type of store it could be. My answer soon came via a warm aromatic smell through the window—it was a coffee house. The warm brew pulled me from my bed and into a cotton summer dress. I pulled my hair back and went bounding down the stairs, eager to get my hands around a cup of java.

"Where are you off to?" Luke asked from the kitchen.

"Oh, hey. I didn't know you were up. The smell of coffee from next door woke me. Do you want me to grab you a cup?"

"No, I already brewed a pot," he answered.

I really wanted the street coffee, but I knew that if I bought a cup now, it would just taste like guilt. So, I turned and walked into the kitchen, poured a cup, and took a deep sip. "Yum," I said to Luke, surprised by its rich taste. "Your coffee is delicious."

"Well, thank you. I aim to please," he replied, holding his cup up to mine. "I thought we could plan the day. Are you up for some sightseeing? Then, we need to go to the grocery. We're having a little dinner party."

"Oh, are we? That sounds fun."

"It should be. And I think you'll really like our guests. Let's get dressed and get an early start."

And what will we be serving?"

"What do you know how to make?" he asked.

I thought for a second. I had cooked often enough for my sister and me in New York, but since I'd been back in Savannah, I had eaten almost every meal with my parents or at Aggie's. "I can make grilled cheese sandwiches, chicken parmesan, and meatloaf."

Luke turned up his nose. "A loaf of meat? No, no, no! Claude always prepares the meals for my parties. He once was a famous chef."

"Very nice. That's a big relief for me. So, what do we need to pick up in the store?"

"Just some wine, Claude's getting everything else from the market."

We chatted as we moved along the streets. He would point out things as we passed but didn't stop until we came to the entrance to the pope's palace. "Do you know there once was a time when the pope lived in France?" he asked.

"Seems like I remember learning that in high school. Is this the place?" Jan asked excitedly.

"Yes, this is the place. The influence of the French government pulled the papal headquarters from Rome to Avignon. Seven popes lived right here in the 1300s until St. Catherine of Siena traveled to Avignon, lived here for months, and finally convinced Gregory XI to return the papacy to Rome."

Jan smiled at him. "You sound like you might have heard that story a few times."

"I did tell you my parents were curators here, right? Well, as a teenager, I helped give tours. It was actually some of the famous artwork inside that built my love of art. Let me show you around the largest Gothic building of the Middle Ages." He took her to many places inside that even the tour guides were unaware of. He hadn't been back inside the palace in years. He had forgotten how much he'd missed it. These were his stomping grounds growing up, and he was happy to be back.

Leaving the palace, he walked me down the cobbled streets and outside the historic walls before ending at the main square in Avignon named Place de l'Horloge.

"Your city is beautiful, Luke. Thank you for sharing it with me." I looked past him to the many posters hanging around the square. "What are all these?" I asked.

"Flyers for Avignon's Art and Music Festival."

"Can we go?"

"Of course. It runs all month. I've got a local pass. We can go to whatever you'd like. The most popular band is playing Saturday night. We should definitely go that night."

"It's a date," I said, unsure what that would mean to Luke.

The wording captured his attention. "Okay. It's a date. But right now, we must be getting home. We have a dinner party to get ready for."

The guests arrived at eight sharp, each ready to be entertained. They seemed surprised that Luke had a date, but even more surprised that I couldn't speak French.

The conversation moved quickly, and they felt no obligation to include me, and certainly no remorse. At first, I was upset. Not as much at them, but at Luke. He had tried to keep me in their conversation at first, but after a while, he gave up. It was too hard to stay in the present while explaining it to me. I thought of Christine telling me that if I were to live in France, I should try harder to speak the language, so I concentrated on words and tried to connect. I was happy when Claude called the group to the table for dinner. At least now, I could be distracted by the food on my plate.

I smiled through the first course, but by the time dessert was served, I decided to disappear. No one seemed to notice as I slid out of my chair and left the room. And if they did, it didn't affect them because to them, I was insignificant.

I snuck upstairs to my room, grabbed my small sketchpad and pencils, then returned to the gathering. I found a chair in the corner, nestled between the red bookshelf and a large paned window. The fabric was worn with age. I could almost picture the readers who had snuggled up in its lap, possibly listening to the rain as it hit the window while they traveled on many adventures between the pages of the books.

I decided to take the chair on a little test drive. I shimmied myself into the slight indent of the seat, propped my feet on its matching ottoman, and pulled open my sketchpad. I studied each of the eight guests. I watched their movements, their facial expressions, the way they carried themselves, and their serious-ness or playfulness. Then, one by one, I drew them. I exagger-ated their assets. One had a beautiful smile; another, a well-kept mustache; and one had an incredible cleavage line that she tried hard to show off. After I had the person just the way I liked, I added personal items that came to my mind. A parasol, galoshes, a wide-brimmed hat, whatever it was that made them unique. I completed my last sketch just as the group began to collect their things to leave, so I gathered my sketches and walked towards the door.

Luke seemed surprised to see me. Had he forgotten I was there, or was he just happy I hadn't interrupted him with my inability to speak his native tongue? No matter, I had enjoyed my evening immensely.

As the guest made their way to the door, I stopped each of them and handed them their sketch. "Where I come from, you welcome outsiders and show great hospitality. I wanted to share that with each of you. Thank you for welcoming me to Avignon."

Luke's eyes widened, thinking I was reprimanding his friends. He moved quickly, glancing at each drawing to soften the blow of anything I'd drawn. Instead, he found eight very happy friends, sharing the wonderful images of themselves with each other. I couldn't get a read on Luke. Although he was smiling on the surface, his face showed something else—annoyance. Was he angry not to be the center of attention for the first time that evening? Some people have a hard time sharing the spotlight, but I hadn't pegged him for that type.

As the last guest left, he grabbed me in a hug and spun me around. "You were wonderful tonight, my dear," he said excitedly, then he kissed me. It was the most unromantic kiss I'd ever received—cold and awkward. The taste of wine and cigarettes burned my mouth as I pulled back abruptly.

"What was that?" I asked.

"That was a small taste of what a great couple we could make together," he said confidently.

He must not have noticed the expression on my face as he moved towards me once again. His lips were on my neck before I could wedge my hands between us. I took a step back, and then another one as he continued to approach. "Tell me you haven't thought about what it would feel like to be with Luke Dupris?" he said with slurred words. Then he reached toward me and ran his fingers along my necklace. "I've been dying to see what trinket was lucky enough to hang between your beautiful breasts," he whispered as I continued to back away. I was shocked when he stopped. He froze, holding my medal between his fingers. He held it for a brief moment before letting it fall from his grasp. Shaking his head, he backed away.

I wasn't sure what was going on. He took large gulps of air as his face turned stark white. Was he having a heart attack? I almost didn't care after what he just pulled, but I couldn't stand there and do nothing.

"Luke, are you okay?"

Looking me in the eyes, he whispered, "Eliana?"

He was delusional. "No, it's me, Jan."

"I'm so sorry, Eliana. I'm so sorry," he said through a gut-wrenching cry, then he ran out of the room.

Chapter 24

Abandoned

Luke paced back and forth, trying to make sense of it all. "What just happened?" he muttered over and over, trying to find the reason behind his madness.

It had been a perfect night. A night that had felt like the dinner parties he and Eliana had given when she was with him in Avignon. He had visited with his friends, enjoyed several bottles of delicious wine, and shared a magnificent meal. Jan had been the perfect hostess. She helped with the meal and mingled on her own. She wasn't like the other women he had tried to host with. Jan hadn't required his attention, so he had been free to have fun.

She had surprised him when she offered the little pictures to his friends as they left. He thought she was just trying to show off her skills, but he humored her by viewing each one. It was something about those pictures. What was it? He hadn't put the pieces together at that time. It was a deep memory his subconscious had filed away. But here it was, coming to the surface.

Leaning onto the foot of the bed, he let his memories

unfold back to the time when he was a young wannabe artist. It had always been his goal to be good enough to sit among the many artists in the public square, Place Du Tertre. He had finally mustered up his nerve that morning to travel to the outskirts of Paris to Montmartre. He had arrived at first light, just as the restaurants were receiving their shipments and the early risers were hustling their way to Sacre Couer for seven a.m. Mass. He set up his easel, arranged his supplies, and opened a tiny stool that was much too short for his easel. No one else was around, so he went in search of a cup of café au lait. When he returned, all of his supplies had been scooted down to the very end of the row of artists. He began to protest but was met with dead stares. So, he had settled into his new spot.

He watched her cross the square, stumbling over the large easel. He smiled, knowing he had done the same, but there had been no one watching. He glanced at the other artists, who nudged one another, snickering under their breaths. He went to help her, but she shook her head as he approached. "I must do this myself," she snipped, then added, "but thank you."

She managed to make it to the spot past him, at the very end, then dropped all of her supplies to the ground. It surprised him when she began to laugh. It was a contagious sound that somehow melted his heart. He looked forward to getting to know her better. Surely, they would have plenty of time to talk; two young artists at the end of the row would never get any attention. But that day, she was on top of the world.

She was like no other artist in the square. People were drawn to her, but they all watched from afar as she created. She'd pick them out of the crowd and see something in each person that no one else saw, possibly something they didn't even see in themselves. Then, she'd set each drawing on the cobbled stones as she finished. She'd look at her subject and say,

"It's yours. Leave for me what you'd like," then move on to her next pick.

Luke's eyes widened. That's exactly what Jan did tonight. She had that same observant eye. His hands began to shake as his breath quickened, but he made himself go back to that memory from the past.

The crowds had continued around Eliana that day until the sun began to set. At that point, she had set her last sketch on the ground and closed her sketch pad. She had searched for him, and when their eyes met, she broke out in the same mesmerizing laugh that had caught his attention in the first place. If he was honest with himself, he fell in love with her the instant he heard her laugh. He could still picture her in that moment.

His hand went to his chest as he felt the familiar heartache, but his mind quickly jumped back into the present. "What have I done?" he whispered, picturing himself advancing on Jan. He had been drawn to her, like a moth to a flame. He finally gave in to it and kissed her. He knew the moment it happened that he had gone too far. He could hear Jorge reminding him to know his boundaries. But his boundaries had become skewed the moment she began to tug on her lip. That's when he made his mistake and moved in closer instead of backing away. He pulled the necklace from her shirt before fully realizing that Jan, from the States, was just as powerful as Eliana was. And now, he had to get away.

He hurriedly began to pack, knowing he was running but not sure from what. He stopped only for a brief second to pen a letter to Jan and slip it under her door before waking Claude to drive him into Paris.

Chapter 25

The Rocker

I woke up still angry with Luke. I was going to give him a piece of my mind today. As my feet hit the floor, I noticed a piece of paper in front of the door. It must have been slipped under my bedroom door in the middle of the night.

Jan,

Something came up in the city that cannot wait. Please stay as long as you'd like at the flat and please take this time to see all of Provence. You won't be sorry.

Luke

Something came up in the middle of the night between the time he called me by his dead wife's name and the first light of dawn? Bullcrap. He's a coward and can't face his mistakes. My face burned with fury. He left me in a foreign country where I don't speak the language. Alone. That was inexcusable!

Walking to the window, I opened it and let the early morning street sounds fill my ears. Thoughts of the night before ran through my mind. He called me Eliana. In my experience, it's never good to be called by another woman's name. Multiply that by a thousand when it's that person's dead wife. Strangely enough, the worst part was how he looked at me. He seemed almost scared. I hadn't said or done anything weird. Honestly, I was just trying to get away from him. But he kept coming at me. Maybe I should have been more vocal. Or instead of retreating, stood my ground and told him to back off. It's funny how I always have these great ideas after the fact.

I still couldn't believe I agreed to come to France with him. Something about that night at Pinkie's made me feel like being adventurous. I'm sure the fact that he was a big superstar had a small part in my decision, too. I had even found him attractive. Now, all that was gone.

I took a deep breath after my mental rant and the strangest sensation filled me—relief. *He's gone. Now, I'm not forced to have an awkward conversation about last night. And I can wander the town and sketch. I have a place to stay, a stocked kitchen, and tickets to the many shows and concerts at the festival all month. I have no one to answer to. I need no one's approval on what I draw. I can just be me.*

I got dressed, grabbed my sketchbook, and headed out to find adventure. I walked and walked, sketching, snacking, and meeting the people on the streets. The locals in Avignon were kind and very accommodating. They tried to communicate with me, almost to a fault, sometimes leading me to places I had no business being. One of them was an empty neighborhood plaza. I had just purchased an ice cream and was trying to ask the store's owner about the location of the concert that evening. The owner gave me directions to a neighborhood plaza just around the corner.

When I arrived, there was no one there. Still, it was a beautiful square, lined by the back side of a row of houses, so I decided to sit on one of the benches and enjoy my ice cream.

The smell of food wafted from the house's windows, no doubt from the many dinner tables inside. The sounds of everyday family life filled the air. I quietly licked my ice cream, wondering how it would feel to sit at the table with one of the families. But instead, it was just me and the hundreds of pigeons that had accumulated, sitting in the park, envious of those inside.

Before I knew what was happening, a man walked to the park's center. He opened a table and began taking items out of a box. Within a minute, he was ready to perform. He caught my eye, nodded, then began. As soon as "Born to be Wild" started blasting from a boom box, his hands began to move. Two cat marionettes danced with all their might, jumping and jiving to the music.

I'm not sure why, but my emotions overcame me. At first, I was bouncing with the music, politely trying to sing along. But as the first song ended, the sounds of an accordion filled the square with a beautiful French tune. As nightfall set in, locals slowly began to drift onto the square. Kids approached the puppeteer to dance with the cats, and one couple began to spin around to the music.

I felt a tear run down my face. I longed for my family and friends and my sweet hometown of Savannah. Why had I left? I could barely remember. What was I trying to prove by traveling this far? As soon as I asked, I remembered how my art had come alive while being here. I had accomplished what I had come to do. But somehow in the process, I had gotten mixed up in Luke's problems. Maybe it was time to go home.

When I popped the last bite of the waffle cone in my mouth, I stood to leave but had suddenly lost all sense of direction. I noticed a trail of people walking down a certain path, leaving the square, so I followed. As the walkway turned into a larger street, the number of people became denser until the street ran into the main city square. I remembered it from my tour with Luke. It was the square where the headliners in the festival played.

I found a seat on the edge of a large planter in the back and listened along. The band had a great sound, but their best quality was that they were singing in English. My ears relished the sound of good old rock & roll.

At the end of the set, the leader announced the band members by name. One by one, each told where in England they were born. Then the band leader came to the last one, he hushed the crowd and said, "Filling in for our regular guitarist, welcome Eddie Simon from the United States."

I jumped down from the planter to get a better look as I watched the young man from the plane walk center stage and wave to the crowd. I smiled. Had I really blown him off at the airport? And for what, a crazy artist? The universe had given me a second chance, and I was going to hold onto it this time, with both hands.

Making my way toward the stage, I slowly inched closer until I finally found a sliver of opportunity and jumped in. I was directly in front of him. I sang along loudly, completely enjoying myself, until I felt his stare. When our eyes met, his face lit up. I had questioned if he would even recognize me, but now all doubts flew out the window. He kept playing while moving toward the side of the stage. A man appeared out of nowhere and leaned toward Eddie as he told him something, then the man looked over at me and nodded. A few minutes later, I was standing next to that man backstage, knowing I had finally found the adventure I'd set out for that morning.

The concert ended in a spectacle of lights and pyrotechnics. I covered my ears while I scanned the hundred-year-old buildings. My eyes moved from the crowd, who were cheering and clapping along to the finale, and then up to the buildings in the square. Their windows may have shaken a little, but this was nothing compared to the action they had seen over the years. They had withstood bombings in World War II and several altercations before that.

Thousands of people were packed in this square for the festival's main event, and everyone was screaming with excitement. I turned my attention back to Eddie just in time to watch him play his last chord, then throw his hands in the air as the crowd went wild. A man from the stage crew leaned over and yelled, "We gotta go."

The band ran off in one direction, while the people on the sidelines exited in the other direction. The stage crew was rushing on to clean up as we were rushing off. The crowd continued to cheer, falling into a joint clapping chant of "Encore!" Sadly, the band never heard their plea. They had already run into the building designated for them. I followed.

I was pushed inside a long hallway while the outside doors were closed quickly behind us, just in time.

What am I doing here? I wondered when the fans began to beat on the door. *This is madness.*

Then I heard my name being called. As soon as I found the source, I knew why I was there—Eddie. My stomach flip-flopped as he approached. He grabbed me and spun me around. The sweat from his body was wet against my sundress, but somehow I wasn't repulsed. His energy was contagious as his adrenaline still pumped through his body from the performance.

"I'd love to take you to dinner if you can give me five minutes to shower off?" he said.

"I'd love that," I answered.

A huge smile spread across his face, making my stomach drop for the second time. He gave me a quick kiss on the lips and ran off. I watched him disappear down the hall as people moved back and forth all around him. True to his word, five minutes later, we snuck out the back door of the building and down one of the many side streets.

Eddie excitedly talked about the show, the mistakes he made, and the backstage fire during the light show finale. I laughed along, relishing his excitement. He was still telling me stories from the night when we arrived at the restaurant.

"I ate here last night. They had the best steak I've eaten since I've been in France," he shared.

When the hostess informed us they were full for the evening, he was visibly disappointed. Thankfully, the owner recognized Eddie from the previous night.

"Eddie, *mona mi.* Come. Come," he said as he patted him on his shoulder. The tall man escorted us through the restaurant, out the back door, and onto a terrace. "This is where all my friends dine," he said before walking away. The owner must have been very popular judging by the twelve tables full of friends.

We were each brought a small carafe of wine and some bread and then we were forgotten about. We sipped and talked while picking at the round, sourdough loaf. When I poured my last glass of *vin*, the waiter reappeared. "Our special," he said while placing a plate in front of us. I almost complained, until the waiter announced, "Braised Lamb shank with lemon confit and sweet pearl onions served with mushroom risotto and roasted vegetables. *Bon appétit.*"

It was the best meal I had experienced since arriving in France. The food was delicious, but the company made it even more enjoyable. Eddie had a way of putting me at ease. He talked without any reservations, but more than that, he listened attentively.

I told him about Luke and being left in Avignon. He immediately became protective of me, which was endearing but unnecessary. "I'm fine," I reassured him. "I have a nice place to stay and a ticket back to Paris."

"Are you ready to go back to Paris?" he asked.

"Not quite yet. I want to see Provence while I'm here."

He only paused a moment before saying, "I've got a few days off before I need to meet up with the band in Paris. Let's see Provence together. I've been told that I must see the lavender fields. I'm not sure what they are, but I'd love to go if you're game."

"Yes!" I blurted out far too quickly. I felt the excitement run through my body. I don't think I'd realized how worried I had been by being alone in a foreign country.

Eddie paid the bill and asked if I was ready to leave. When I nodded, he stood. "Let's meet for coffee in the morning to plan our time here," he said.

"Sounds good," I answered, then added, "Thank you for dinner. I had a great night."

Eddie laughed. "This date isn't over; we were just refueling. I hope you're ready to do some dancing."

I gave him a serious look that made him stop in his tracks. Using my best Southern twang, I said, "I'm from Savannah, Georgia. We are always ready to dance. Lead the way!"

He laughed loudly. It was the kind of laugh that makes others smile, too. It was genuine. Just like the man himself.

Chapter 26

Provence

Our morning coffee morphed into a late lunch after staying out late in the clubs. I had no idea that the historic city of Avignon would have so many dancing spots. My feet ached.

Eddie showed up at the flat with two sandwiches and a map. We found a shaded bench to sit on and people-watched while we ate. Then, we spread the map out to make a plan.

"Provence is such a large area. It goes all the way to the Mediterranean Sea," I remarked.

"Yes. We definitely can't see everything in two days. But we can cram in a lot," he replied.

I nodded. "Yes. Or we could take our time and wander, spending as much time as we'd like in the places we land."

He smiled. I turned my attention back to the map but felt his eyes still on me. Slowly, I met his stare. He didn't look away.

"What?" I asked.

"I just like the way you think, that's all."

"Oh, that's all?" I asked.

"No. I think you're cute and I like being with you."

I paused. What I was about to do made me feel vulnerable. "I like being with you, too. And I guess you're pretty easy on the eyes," I said, feeling the sting of a blush make its way onto my cheeks.

"You guess?"

"Don't push your luck."

He laughed. I could get used to hearing that laugh every day. We did seem to click. I had noticed that the first time we met. He was flirty, yet intentional. He was a welcome change from my loneliness in Avignon.

He pulled the map back open and we both leaned in, studying the bright tourist spots, each pointing to the places we'd like to see. Eddie decided he would rent a car and we'd leave first thing the following morning.

We spent the first day town hopping. We began by visiting the hilltop village of Gordes. Its limestone buildings and cobblestone streets were enchanting. We took our time meandering around the town, then made our way to the next stop.

Roussillon is famous for its red hues. Built among ochre cliffs, nearly every building is a shade of red. Being a Georgia girl, I was familiar with red clay. Still, a whole red village was something to marvel at.

Next, we drove to the medieval city of Les Baux-de-Provence, chatting the whole drive about our favorite things we'd seen so far. We walked through the charming village but spent most of our time exploring the castle and its ruins, which dated back thousands of years. The limestone was hard to travel upon as we climbed to the top of the fortress. But once there, we had a view of all of Provence.

I spun around, enjoying every angle. I glanced at Eddie, who had found a seat on a large chunk of rock. He was flipping through a brochure he had picked up in the town.

"They say there was a human settlement on this site in

6000 B.C. That's over 8,000 years ago. I can't wrap my head around that."

I sat down beside him and leaned my head on his shoulder to get a better view of the brochure that he was so engrossed in. I barely glanced at it before saying, "I think my brain's on overload. Are you about ready to head back?"

He seemed surprised but not upset. "We've seen a lot. But can you hang in there for one more stop?" he asked. When I nodded, he added, "Then let's get a move on before we lose sunlight."

This time, the car ride was made in silence. Not a bad silence, but the quietness of two people who were tired but still content to be traveling along together. We arrived relatively quickly at our last stop, Pont du Gard. We walked up to the entrance and bought tickets just as the last tour guide was stepping away with a group. He motioned for us to join, so we jumped in.

"The Pont du Gard is the best-preserved Roman remains in the world. The three-tiered aqueduct bridge was built in the first century. It delivered 11,000,000 gallons of water daily from springs in Uzès to the homes in Nimes, which was over thirty miles away." The guide continued to talk as the aqueduct came into view.

When the group moved in one direction towards the bottom of the structure, Eddie went another route. He followed the signs to the footpath leading to the bridge on the aqueduct. He hurried along, like a little kid, while excitedly restating the facts the guide had just shared. "The first century? How were the Romans so smart? Look at the enormity of this. How has it stood this long?"

I followed behind, trying to keep up, until we actually stepped onto the bridge. We marveled at the size of the archways above, strategically placed without using mortar, as we walked to the center of what was once a fierce river below. My thoughts jumped to Stephanie, wondering if she had seen this site when she studied abroad. It truly was an architect's dream.

I was surprised when Eddie stopped suddenly. "We just made it!" he said excitedly while pointing to the sunset. We wandered over to the edge, leaning on the large limestone blocks as the sky turned to orange. I was surprised when he wrapped his arm around my shoulder. I snuck a look up at his face as he stared out over the canyon. He stood proud, like a man who had conquered the world.

"What are you thinking about right now?" I prepared for a deep and philosophical reply during his long pause.

He deepened his voice and answered, "I am Gladiator." He then dropped his arm from my shoulder, balled up his fist, and hit his chest hard before raising his voice even louder. "My name is Maximus Decimus Merdius, Commander of the Armies of the North and General of the Felix Legions, loyal servant to the true emperor, Marcus Aurelius."

His face remained stern. I looked around at the people standing on the bridge. All eyes were on us. When everyone began to clap, he exhaled and began to smile. The cheers continued as he took a bow. One man even called out, "Yeah, man! *Gladiator* is the best!" He turned to me and bowed again. I clapped but had no idea what had just happened. He saw the confusion on my face.

"That was from *Gladiator*. You know, the movie?"

No, I didn't know. "Did you have to learn that for school or something?"

"School? No, I just watched the movie a lot, that's all."

I didn't have brothers, and let's just say my dad's not the type of person who would watch a bloody movie, so I couldn't relate. But I knew it would hurt his feelings if I didn't respond. So, I did what most women do when they don't understand something a man does—lie. "That was amazing. You nailed it. However, I really didn't see that coming when I asked what's on your mind."

"I like to keep you guessing," he replied. "But seriously, the Romans did great things."

"Yeah, like kill all the Christians in Rome?"

"Not their finest moment. But look at this. They paved the way to modern civilization."

"Yes, maybe. But I'm more impressed that they did these things while wearing a dress."

"It was a tunic, but yes. Don't judge." He grabbed me by the waist, pulling me closer. "Thank you for agreeing to one more stop today. This one was my favorite."

"Thank you for being honest about what you were actually thinking earlier." I thought for only a brief second before adding, "You would have made a very sexy gladiator."

He leaned down, his hand moving behind my neck as he steadied me for one of the greatest kisses of my life. Our lips seemed to be made for one another. When I finally pulled back, he said, "Wow, I didn't see that coming," just as I had earlier.

And I answered just as he had. "I like to keep you guessing."

Chapter 27

Lavender Fields

Eddie was late. Truth be told, I had kept him up until the wee hours of the morning. Still, it was our last day together. *If he really liked me, he wouldn't have over-slept,* I told myself. My mind was always cross in the face of disappointment. Although, he had at least called to tell me he was running behind.

I began to pack my things for my trip back to Paris. I had picked up gifts for the tribe—scarves, decorative tiles, and a papal flag for Kathleen and Jack. I couldn't fit everything in my bag. I made a mental note to purchase a tote while I was out today.

When I heard the knock, I opened the door to a very apologetic Eddie.

"No time for apologies, lavender fields await," I answered.

His smile at being let off the hook made me weak in the knees before my mind cautioned me. *Can I trust him not to break my heart?*

The ride to the fields took about an hour. We found a radio station playing '80s music and sang along. I was surprised by his voice. "I didn't know you could sing, too. I thought you were a guitarist only."

"Yes, ma'am. I can sing. I've even sang on stage at the Grand Ole Opry."

"No way!"

"I did. My dad had a friend who wrote jingles and he always got me to play them to make sure the key was correct. One day, they asked him onto the Grand Ole Opry and he took me along. It was the best night of my life."

"That's quite an accomplishment at your age, Eddie. What a thrill. But was it really the best night of your life?"

He reached over and grabbed my hand. "Nah, it was the second-best night of my life."

I began to say, "Aww," but he interrupted me. "Meeting Clint Black and Dolly Parton at the after-party was the first."

I slapped him on the shoulder, causing him to laugh. He would always get me with that laugh. Eventually, I joined in.

He pointed to a sign ahead marked D6, and we turned onto the highway. Within a couple of miles, we were surrounded by lavender fields. They ran down both sides of the road and were fenced off from the public. I began to notice cars stopped along the fence with people getting their picture taken with a sea of purple backdrop.

"You know what I call those people?" I asked.

"What?"

"Quitters. Let's keep driving until we hit fields we can run in. I need to get underneath a lavender plant."

"What exactly does that mean?"

"You see, my grandfather painted a picture of the lavender, but his point of view seemed to be from lying underneath the stalks. It's always baffled me, so that's what I want to do, too.

He thought for a moment. "Okay, then, we shall move

forward," he exclaimed, holding his hand in front of him as if he were holding a sword.

"Gladiator?" I asked.

"Uh, maybe," he answered and continued to drive. We went about ten more minutes until Eddie turned sharply down a small drive. "I think we need to get off the main road if we want to find you a plant to climb under," he explained as the road got bumpy. Eddie slowed the car to a crawl, maneuvering around large holes in the dirt road. When he finally saw a small clearing, he parked the car.

"Let's go," he said, quickly unbuckling his seatbelt.

"We can't just go into someone's field."

"Look around. They have hundreds of acres of fields. What are they gonna do, arrest us for climbing under one of their plants?" he asked.

I laughed. "No, I guess not."

"Then come on," he said as he stepped out of the car.

I followed until we were standing at the end of a row. A gentle breeze moved the stems back and forth, releasing their sweet fragrance. I was mesmerized. I don't even know what came over me, but I began to run. I could hear Eddie calling out behind me, but I didn't stop. I just ran, tripping and stumbling over the loose soil. I didn't stop until I ran out of breath and collapsed onto the soft, tilled soil. Then, I rolled over onto my back and looked up into a scene so familiar that I could almost tell you the direction of every petal. I'd seen it a hundred times before in my grandfather's painting. I felt the tears before I knew I was crying. My grandfather had been in one of these lavender fields off of D6. Once again, I was connected to him. Suddenly, it didn't matter if Luke had left me alone in Avignon. Eddie had brought me exactly where I needed to be. I was there in my grandfather's painting.

Eddie finally caught up with me. "What the hell was that?" he asked, kneeling beside me.

I reached up and placed my arms around his neck, then pulled him next to me. I gently rolled him onto his back. Seeing the want in his eyes, I slowly shook my head no and lay down next to him instead. "Look," I said, pointing up to the lavender above. "I had to get under the lavender."

"Oh! Now I get it."

"My grandfather Gerard was from France. He was a great artist and shared that love with me. He has two paintings that I loved. I found where the first one was painted in Montmartre. Now I've found the place where the second one was painted, too—the lavender fields on D6."

Eddie found my hand and laced his fingers into mine. We lay with our heads touching, looking up through the purple haze of flowers and straight up to the blue sky. Neither of us spoke as the sweet and earthy scent of lavender enveloped us; we were both just present in the moment.

The next thing I knew, I opened my eyes to total darkness. Fear engulfed me. It took a moment to remember where I was. *Why am I alone?* Terrified, I reached over and let out a sigh of relief when my hand hit Eddie's. "Eddie? Eddie?" I called out, shaking him awake.

"What? I can't see a thing. There's something crawling on me," he yelled and jumped up.

I jumped up, too, and began to run my hands all over my body and through my hair to get any insects off of me.

"Never mind, it was just flowers hitting my leg."

I began to breathe easier.

"I've never known darkness like this," he said.

"I know. Look at those stars."

"Where is the moon? How will we find our way back to the car?"

Just then, a yellow flashing light began to spin in the distance. "Let's follow that light," I suggested. So, we did. We tripped a few times and fell into several of the bushes, but once we found ourselves in a row, the path became a little easier to follow. We continued along the row until we came to the flashing light of the tow truck, pulling away with our vehicle.

"Wait! Wait!" Eddie called out. The truck slammed on the brakes. Eddie tried to explain that it was his car that was being towed, but the driver didn't understand any English. Finally, he motioned us into the cab of the truck.

Climbing into the bed of the truck, I settled in the middle of the long leather seat, covered in papers and wrappers. The driver grunted and began to scold me in French while motioning to the seat beneath me. Eddie pulled me towards him as the man dislodged a bag from where I had been sitting. He then pulled out the contents of a sandwich, or what was once a sandwich, to show me why he was so upset.

"I'm sorry," I said repeatedly, but he kept shaking his head. Noticing his business license pasted to the dashboard with the name "Vern" and his photo, I decided to try something else. I lowered my voice and called him by name. "Vern, I'm sorry," I said, then put my hands together like I was praying.

The face that had been so upset slowly moved into a smile, then he waved me off and turned on the radio. French tunes filled the truck bed and escaped out our open windows as we traveled down the bumpy, dirt road. The warm summer air, filled with scents of lavender, circled us. I breathed it in. Eddie reached over and pulled two small twigs of lavender from my hair. "One for you and one for me," he said, "for us both to remember the night we slept together in a lavender field."

I smiled, savoring the moment, knowing I would never forget my favorite night in France.

Chapter 28

Finish to the End

"Janine, look harder," I heard my grandfather say. "Can't you see it?"

"See what?" I mumbled, the sound of my voice stirring me. Turning on my side, I struggled to open my eyes, but the sliver of light shining on the pale blue wall was blinding and made me retreat back to the darkness behind my eyelids.

"Can't you see it? Look harder." I could still hear his voice in the distance as the image of the day I had found him painting in the corner of his garden crept into my dream-like state.

"May I?" I had asked, eager to see what the canvas held. When he nodded, I walked around to the front, only this time it wasn't the painting of his boyhood playground. This time, it was Luke's most well-known painting. The first one that brought him into the public eye: *Ascend*.

I shot out of bed. "Where are all the paintings Luke is working on?" I mumbled as I grabbed my jeans off the floor and slid them over my hips. I could almost hear Luke's voice as I ran down the hallway. "The guest rooms are upstairs and each door is open. There are three to choose from. I have an office up there, too, that I rarely use so I locked it off." I remembered wondering why anyone felt they should lock a door inside their own house unless they had something to hide.

I walked down the hall toward the office. I might as well give it a try, I thought. Reaching for the doorknob, I gave it a turn and wasn't surprised to find it locked, just as Luke had said. It was then that I remembered the keys sitting in the dish beside the front door.

I hurriedly descended the staircase, making more noise than usual. When I reached the bottom, I turned down the hallway and ran right into Claude. He looked me over suspiciously, or at least that's what my subconscious was telling me.

"*Bonjour,*" I sing-songed to him.

"*Bonjour,*" he grunted in reply as he pushed past me down the hallway.

I quietly retrieved the keys and tiptoed back up the stairs. The keyring held about ten keys. I was surprised when the third one turned the lock. Entering the room, I flipped on the overhead light, but it helped very little. Old flats such as this were known for their bad lighting. I slowly closed the door behind me and stepped deeper into the room.

I had found it odd that Luke would put his office in the only room without a window, but as I looked around, it began to make sense. The darkness covered his secret. I walked along the walls slowly, viewing the many paintings that were hanging. They were lovely landscapes and still lifes. Some had the blur of a person in the background, but the main focus was on the scene itself.

After viewing each picture, I then walked back around, focusing on his signature. Luke had signed his name exactly the same in each one. He used an exaggerated L that trailed off to an exaggerated D, followed by a small p before trailing off once again.

Why had he hidden all his work away? *None of this makes sense*, I thought. Then the image of Luke's most famous painting hit me. It's almost as if...

My thought was interrupted by the sound of someone stomping up the stairs. I flipped off the light and stood very still. That's when I noticed I had forgotten to lock the door. If those clod-like steps belonged to Claude, he would know that the door stayed locked.

The stomping on the stairs had stopped. Someone was shuffling down the hallway. I turned the lock slowly, so as not to make any noise. I felt the lock catch just as someone on the other side turned the handle. Startled, I jumped back, my hand flying to my mouth to cover up any sound. Everything was completely quiet.

I didn't move a muscle until I heard footsteps moving along. The person walked down the hall, then passed back by the office before walking back downstairs. Then, I heard the front door close. I scanned the room one last time before leaving the office, locking the door behind me.

When I returned the keys to where they lived, in the glass bowl on the foyer table, I found a note with my name on it.

> Dear Jan,
>
> I can't stop thinking about our weekend together. It was amazing experiencing Provence with you. I look forward to the time when our paths cross once again.
>
> Eddie

Wait. That was Eddie I heard upstairs? I bolted out the front door and searched both ways on the street, but there was no sign of him. Stomping my foot down hard, I grunted, "Damn!"

The sound of laughter spilling out of the coffee shop broke my anger. My eyes searched for its source, and they landed on Eddie.

"You looking for me?" he called out.

A small smile worked its way across my face, but then I remembered my appearance. I hadn't been awake for very long, yet so much had happened in that short time. Eddie motioned me over to the small table where he sat. I glanced down at my bare feet hanging out of my jeans and my old Mickey Mouse shirt, tattered with age.

"You look fine," he called out, so I walked in his direction. He stood and gave me a small peck on my cheek. I was grateful it wasn't more, knowing a toothbrush hadn't found its way into my mouth yet. "Do you stomp your feet often?"

I felt the sting on my cheeks. "Not often, but more than I want to admit," I answered.

"Well, I'm happy to see that I got such a big reaction from you," he said with a knowing smile. He took a sip of his coffee and added, "That big French guy let me in and motioned me upstairs. Where were you?"

My mind tumbled for an answer. I certainly couldn't tell him I was sleuthing around, investigating the person who was allowing me to stay at his beautiful flat for free. That would be very ungrateful of me. Maybe a small lie would be better. "I was in the little girls' room."

"Oh, okay," was all he said. And just like that, my whereabouts were no longer questioned. There was something about men not wanting to know what ladies did when they were in the restroom that kept my secret safe.

"What time does your train leave?"

Eddie glanced down at the table, then met my eyes. "In a couple of hours, but I just had to see you again, Jan. I think we've got something here. I know you feel it, too. I'm not sure what it is, but I really like being with you. Are you sure you won't reconsider coming with me? You could see the rest of France, Scotland, and Ireland, and we could have a blast doing it. Come on. What do you say?"

I wanted to scream YES! But I knew I must go back to Montmartre. There were just too many things I needed to finish. I bravely answered, "There is nothing I'd rather do..." I began, watching a smile form on Eddie's face. I had to finish quickly. "But I have to finish what I started here in France, and that means going back to Montmartre."

"To him?" Eddie asked abruptly.

"It's not like that. I thought you understood."

"I do. Does Luke?"

I placed my hand over his. "You're right about one thing. You and I are a good fit. And I truly hope that we find our way back to each other. But right now, right this minute, is not our time."

He pulled his hand away, turned up his coffee, and set money on the table. Shrugging his shoulders, he muttered, "You can't blame a guy for trying."

When he stood, I did, too. Reaching out for him, I ran my hand down the side of his face. I was half-surprised he didn't pull away. "I'm so happy we found each other in this small town in France. I really hope we find each other again, one day," I whispered.

He leaned in and kissed me softly on the lips and left. I watched as he walked down the small street until he disappeared in the crowd. Part of me wanted to run after him. For whatever reason, Eddie felt like home, and that was a welcome feeling to the isolation I had become accustomed to in France.

But I knew if I left with him, I would be walking away from every reason I had come to France. I had given in to this feeling before in New York. I had given up on drawing for a guy and almost lost everything. But this time, I was going to finish what I started.

Chapter 29

The Hospital

Thoughts of Eliana filled Luke's mind as he took his weekly walk to the cemetery. The memories always came in the same way: Their innocent meeting, her brightness and brilliance, then the slow fade into reclusiveness. He sometimes wondered if he was the one who had killed her. God knows the police still suspected him. And although he hadn't physically shoved her off the cliff, he allowed her slow decline.

He knew he would never be the artist she was. Still, he thought he could watch and learn from her. But instead, she pushed him away and found solace in her studio. Alone. She went from being wonderful to extraordinary, but no one knew. Unlike him, she didn't create to be noticed or for profit. She created because she couldn't imagine her life without a paintbrush in her hand. Every painting was a glimpse into her soul, and no one knew.

People would ask him all the time about the inspiration behind each piece of art, but he had no idea. He always gave a lame explanation about how artists just paint and let the world melt into the canvas. But, like them, he really wished he knew. He wished Eliana had shared that part of her life with him. So, he continued his weekly walk, trying desperately to get inside the brain of his incredibly talented dead wife.

When he returned home, there was a message from the hospital waiting, asking him to come right away.

Luke rushed into the hospital room and was shocked to find Jorge sitting up in bed, eating orange Jello.

"Jorge!" he exclaimed, a little too loudly. "Someone from the hospital left a message for me to come right away. I was worried you took a turn for the worse."

Jorge smiled. "I'm sorry to have worried you, my friend, but I wanted to speak with you before they gave me my next dose of drugs."

Luke gave his friend a hug, trying to be gentle around the many machine wires. He didn't want to bombard him with questions, but he wanted to know the truth. "What happened, Jorge?"

"I'm really not sure. It's all very hazy. But I remember falling. Then, it's all in bits and pieces." Jorge closed his eyes and touched the side of his bandaged head. "It hurts to think right now. I'm sorry."

Luke squeezed his shoulder. "I'm just happy you're okay. We'll have much time to talk later. But right now, you need to rest." He turned to walk out of the room, but Jorge stopped him.

"Not yet. We have some catching up to do. How's our artist friend?"

"Jan?"

"Yes, Jan. Has she settled in?"

Luke thought back. It had been over two weeks since his accident. He wondered if Jorge even knew how long he had been in a coma. He decided to let Jorge lead all conversations. "Yes, Jan has definitely settled in."

"What do you think of her?"

"Jorge, I don't think this is the right time to talk with you. You've only been awake for a short time."

"It's the perfect time to talk with me. Just don't ask me about my fall. That question seems to hurt. I promise, I'll let you know if I get tired. Now, tell me everything."

"Okay. Jan's young. She's beautiful and she's very talented. She spends her days wandering Montmartre and comes back with the most incredible sketches from the past, drawing on how things once appeared as if she could recall that time. They are incredible."

"I didn't ask about her work. I asked about her. Do you have feelings for her?"

"Oh. That's a tricky question. You know how, over the years, every time I begin dating someone, I feel like Eliana is haunting me? I'd catch a glimpse of her or I'd smell her perfume. Well, this time has been the strongest. So, I decided to do the one thing I usually do when I want to get away from her ghost. I escape to Avignon."

"Ah, yes. That was a good idea. Away from your married past."

"Well, I certainly thought so. And we were getting along well. Then one night, I saw the medal hanging around her neck."

"The medal? What medal?"

"Eliana's Miraculous Medal with the ruby trim."

"No. That can't be. You buried her wearing that medal. The sisters told you it was the last one in the family. How could that be?"

Luke ran his hand down his face. "I don't know. I truly don't know."

"What did you do?"

"I stopped what I started. I said goodnight. And the next morning I came home."

"And what about Jan?"

"I left her a note that something came up and for her to stay in Avignon as long as she pleases. I told her to see all of Provence, and when she was ready to come back to Montmartre, to let Claude know and he'd make her arrangements."

"That poor girl, alone in Avignon with Claude. Remember when you left Eliana alone in Avignon?"

"Jan is nothing like Eliana in that sense. She's strong and outgoing. She'll be just fine."

"So how have you been spending your time?"

Luke thought for only a second before answering. "I've been painting. I think we have our new masterpiece. Even Renae agrees."

Jorge moaned and reached for his head just as the nurse entered the room.

"It's time for your medicine, and by the looks of things, you're ready for it," she said as she quickly injected it into the port of his IV. "I'll be back to check on you soon." She then turned to Luke and timidly asked for his autograph on the back of someone's file she was holding.

As she left, Jorge blurted out, "There's more to Jan's story. You have to find out how she came to have that medal."

"Oh, I intend to. But I told her to take her time touring Provence and come back when she's done. I'll talk to her then."

"And you need to warn her," Jorge said with a slur. "She has to know tha..." His words trailed off.

Luke tried to put his last sentence together. Warn her about what? Was there something he wasn't aware of? He needed to get to the bottom of Jorge's fall, and Jorge was the only one with the answers.

Chapter 30

The Next Masterpiece

"Where's Luke?" Renae snipped when she found Christine sitting at his desk.

"He just left for the hospital. Jorge wanted to speak with him. Are you sure you want to be around when he returns?"

"I told you that Jorge stumbled and fell. I am guilty of nothing," she replied.

"Except leaving him for dead. How could you do that? It's starting to sound very familiar," Christine said.

"Be careful. You are treading in deep water," Renae remarked.

"Maybe. But if the police find out you left Jorge, they might start digging around and go back to those open questions surrounding Eliana's death," Christine replied.

"Let them. I did nothing wrong." Renae said as she shuffled papers around on Luke's desk.

Christine took several papers out of Renae's hands and placed them back into the appropriate pile. "On another subject, I think you're going a little overboard with Jan."

"I'm sure I have no idea what you're talking about," Renae answered. The look on Christine's face told her otherwise, so she restated, "Really, I don't."

"Your ghost thing. You've always been so careful and creative with Luke and kept him away from girlfriends for years, but Jan said the ghost has been inside the studio, sometimes even when she's there. That's pretty risky."

"What?" Renae said, leaning in closer on the desk. "I haven't done any of the ghost tricks on her. Why would I want to run her off? We need her to stay and paint."

The color left Christine's face. "Jan's not scared and she's not going anywhere, but she's definitely seeing a ghost."

Renae plopped down in the chair across from Christine. "We certainly can't have something happen to this girl. Have you heard Luke talk about it?"

"No. Jan told me directly. She asked me if the house was haunted. I told her not that I was aware of, but then she explained. I seriously thought it was you. Have you ever felt anything in there before?"

Renae shook her head slowly. "No. But we might be able to use this to our advantage." Her mischievous smile sent more chills down Christine's spine than the thought of an actual haunting. "Keep your ears open. Let me know the next time this happens."

"She's still out of town, but I'll talk to her on her return," Christine remarked.

"Wait. Luke left her in Avignon? So, neither of them is home right now?" Renae asked. Christine shook her head.

"Then we need to go get a look at our young artist's work."

Christine pleaded for Renae not to disturb the studio. She knew how artists felt about intruders and she'd come to respect Jan. But Renae was not to be deterred. And if she was going into Jan's room, Christine was going with her.

A smile spread across her face the second Renae walked through the studio door. "This feels oddly familiar," she murmured. She went from sketch to sketch until she stopped at the painting of the streets of Montmartre. "I think we just found Luke's next masterpiece."

"What are you doing in here?" Luke's stern words made them both jump.

Christine spoke first. "She pushed her way in. I'm sorry, Luke."

Renae turned to Christine. Gritting her teeth together, she whispered, "Is that how we're gonna spin this? Okay." Turning to Luke, Renae answered, "I wanted to see if our young artist was any good. And look what I just found," she said, pointing to the painting.

"I know; it's beautiful. But I told you never to come in here again. Did I not?"

"Yes, yes. But you've already seen this painting? Why didn't you say anything to me?"

Luke shook his head at Renae, then turned to Christine. "Can you please go to my office and pull my itinerary. I'll be in shortly."

Christine nodded and left.

"Shouldn't you be more careful of what you say in front of my assistant, Renae?" Luke chided.

"Of course," she answered. "Now, what about this painting? How can we buy her silence?"

"We're not at that point yet," he answered.

"Well, I'll give you one week to get to that point. Then I'm going to her directly," Renae said, as she pushed past Luke in the doorway.

Luke extended his arm across the doorway to block her way. "You will do no such thing."

Renae didn't back down. Instead, she turned into him. "Try

me," she growled until he dropped his arm, and she left triumphantly.

She couldn't get the image of Jan's painting out of her mind all that afternoon. *This one will be my last one. I'll let Luke do all the dirty work, getting Jan to agree to share her art with him. Then, when it's all said and done, I'll keep all the proceeds. What's Luke going to do, sue me? He could never draw that attention to himself because then he'd have to admit to the world that he's a fake. This last one is all I need to be set for life. I'm tired. I've worked hard all my life. It's time for me to relax and enjoy life a bit. The painting of "The Streets of Montmartre" is my ticket out.*

———

Luke watched Renae walk past the fountain and out of sight. How had he allowed himself to get involved with such a terrible person? And now, he would be asking Jan to get involved, too. He walked into the studio and began to study Jan's art. He was embarrassed that he had only looked at the pieces briefly when she shared them with him in the evenings. It wasn't until he had seen the painting of the children playing in the street that he had taken her seriously. But something had been bothering him, and he couldn't put his finger on it.

One by one, he slowly inspected the sketches until he saw her, deep in the background. Once he spotted the woman, he shuffled to the next canvas and searched. There she was again, and again. In one, she was wearing a large hat. In the next, she was running in the rain under an umbrella. She was the artist sitting on the curb, and in another, she was sitting close to a man on a bench.

His hands began to shake. It was the same woman from the background in Eliana's last painting, *Martyr's Hill*. Eliana had painted herself, and now she had found her way into Jan's art. How could that be?

His grip began to slip as his numb hands set the sketches onto the desk. He half expected to see her ghost himself as he backed out of the studio, but once he made it to the fountain, he let himself collapse into a rocking chair. Eliana wanted him to see these images. She and Jan had a connection, although he wasn't sure why.

He felt the familiar sting of being a second-rate artist, once again. Only this time, he could ask the artist's approval to use her work. It would be awkward, yes, but he would pay Jan so much money that she'd be able to do whatever she wanted. She could travel the world painting or open a gallery in Savannah. He got excited by the idea of Jan being in control of her own future. Now, he just needed to convince her of it.

Chapter 31

———

Permission

Once the train passed through Lyon, I watched the blur of the French countryside. The ride back into Paris felt much different than the voyage down. I could still picture myself studying Luke on the train ride down as he slept, wondering what made him tick. Now, I just wanted to punch him in the face, not only for leaving me alone in Avignon, but for pushing himself on me after the dinner party. It's funny how quickly your opinion of someone can change. Seeing him again was going to be hard.

Claude had informed him that I was coming back, so like it or not, he was expecting me. I couldn't run and hide, and somehow, I didn't want to. I felt like I'd matured in that short week. An image of the office full of his paintings flooded my memories. I'm not sure exactly what was going on with Luke, but I was no longer intimidated by him.

By the time the train pulled into the terminal in Paris, I was prepared. I had decided to act like nothing had happened. Denial was a close friend of mine. I had used it more than I wanted to admit, so it shouldn't be too hard. All I had to do was rewind my brain to the night he took me to dinner at the quaint little restaurant in Montmartre. That's where our story would pick back up. *I'm ready.*

I lugged my heavy bag down the stairs of the train and pulled it across the platform until it reached the main station. That's when I saw Luke. He was balancing a bouquet of flowers in one hand while signing an autograph for a young lady with the other. I briefly considered walking past him when he glanced up. He shooed away his fan and called out my name. "Jan, welcome home." I tried not to cringe when he leaned in and kissed each of my cheeks, lingering a bit too long on each side. Then, he placed the flowers in my free hand.

I told myself to be nice, so I forced a smile and thanked him for the flowers.

"How was your train ride?" he asked.

Nodding my head, I answered, "Very nice; France is lovely."

Small talk. I hate small talk. I'd rather not talk at all. All my self-talk about being calm flew right out the window. I couldn't hold it in anymore. "Why did you leave me in Avignon?" I exploded.

He seemed shocked, but instead of moving away from me, he moved in closer. Taking my elbow, he continued to lead me in the direction of the exit. "Something came up with work," he whispered.

I tried to stop walking to face him, but he continued to lead me along. "That's a lie and we both know it," I said firmly, as we walked through the main doors and out onto the plaza.

He leaned over once more as he searched for the driver. "Let's discuss this in the car, please," he muttered.

I glanced around. People were staring. I had forgotten how he was always in the public eye. Honestly, I no longer looked at him like a celebrity. He was just a person, and a rude person at that. I let him lead me to the car, then slid in the back quietly.

"We have much to discuss," he said softly as the car began to make its way through the city.

"Yes, we do," I whispered, as I watched the hustle and bustle of Paris.

"I have dinner waiting for us at the house," he added.

I only nodded in response, as I continued to look out the window. I suddenly longed to be back in the little town of Avignon. No, I longed to be sitting beside Eddie. The feeling surprised me, but the memory of sitting in the tow truck came flooding back. That was a happy day. And if I were being honest, if Luke had not left me, it never would have happened. I turned to Luke, who was watching me, and answered, "Dinner sounds lovely, thank you." Relief seemed to wash over him as a genuine smile made its way across his face. I could play nice, and a girl's gotta eat.

He had a table set in the backyard, overlooking the city. Liz brought out a tray with cold chicken, sliced potatoes, and a salad, accompanied by a sweet Chenin Blanc. The chilled meal was refreshing in the heat of a summer night.

He asked about my time in Provence, and I told him about my travels, of seeing Gordes, Roussillon, Les Baux-de-Provence, and finally Pont du Gard.

"Oh yes, Pont de Gard. It's one of France's most impressive monuments. The Romans were really something, weren't they?" he asked before hitting his chest.

Before he broke into speech, I interrupted, "*Gladiator* was a great movie, wasn't it?"

He only nodded, but I caught a glimpse of disappointment in his eyes. He turned the conversation back to me. "Did you see the lavender fields?" he asked.

"Of course I did. They were beautiful," I answered. I didn't mention Eddie or my feelings for him. There were some things he didn't need to know. The conversation was light, and I honestly didn't have the energy for it to be more than that. By the end of the meal, I could no longer hide my yawns. I thanked him, went back to the studio, and fell straight into bed.

I woke to the sound of thunder. A bright flash of lightning blinded me through the window as I struggled to open my eyes. I automatically rolled over and turned my back to the light, but the room roared behind each flash. I began to count: one thousand one, one thousand...Boom. The storm was drawing near. Realizing I'd never be able to fall back asleep, I got out of bed and decided to watch it pass from the covered courtyard.

Watching the storm move across the Paris skyline was mesmerizing. I could almost picture the people roaming the streets in the city that never sleeps. They would look up to the sky, and although they had perfect warning from the thunder and lightning, they still seemed surprised when the sky opened up to a downpour. I contemplated running back inside to begin drawing the scene going through my mind, but the sudden drop in temperature held me in place. A large gust transported the smell of rain my way. It was moving quickly. I sat quietly, almost reverently. If the storm didn't see me, it might let me watch without chasing me inside. The rain came hard; tiny bullets exploding into the fountain. But the show ended quickly, and soon I was left with a damp face and wet toes. The world was silent and peaceful.

I'm not sure how long I sat. I must have fallen asleep. A creaking sound woke me. My eyes scanned the dark and focused on my cottage door standing ajar. Had I not shut it when I walked outside? I couldn't remember. Pulling myself up from the large chaise lounge, I stretched and then walked in that direction. A strange feeling came over me, making me stop. Was someone watching me? I looked over my shoulder, then back to the courtyard, before running into the cottage and shutting the door. As I turned the lock, I relaxed a bit into the door. I was safe inside. But that moment of solitude passed quickly as the smell of lavender filled the air. I was not alone. She was there with me, and I had just locked myself inside with her.

I hurried to the lamp next to the sofa, hoping the light would scare her away. My hands awkwardly climbed its base until I found the switch. I turned it once, but nothing happened. I kept turning over and over, but only darkness remained. Had the storm knocked the electricity out while I was outside? I felt a breath on my neck. Shrugging my shoulders in response, I turned, but nothing was there. A chill ran up my spine, but something else came over me. Courage. I was alive and breathing and she was not. I took in a deep breath, and in the steadiest voice I could muster, I said, "I know you're here. I don't wish to intrude in your space, but I'll only be here for a bit before going back to my home in the United States. Like you, I'm an artist and I'd like to create my drawings here, too, if you will permit it."

Light instantly flooded the room from the lamp I had been fiddling with. Had the power come back on, or had I received the answer I'd been hoping for? Either way, I was safe, and I had permission to paint in this studio—by all those living and not living in this house.

Chapter 32

Miraculous Medal

After waking up early that morning, I decided to attend the seven a.m. Mass at Sacre Coeur. The walk from Luke's home to the church was peaceful. There was only one other person walking ahead of me this dark morning. I prayed they were also a Mass goer as I followed behind. I still hadn't mastered all the twists and turns of the small walkways and was grateful to be following someone else. My prayers were answered as the large white dome came into view.

That's when I passed through Place du Tertre square. It was strange to find it empty. Workers were taking the chairs off the tables where they had been stored the night before, ready for the next day of patrons. I stopped for a brief moment, trying to let each corner of the square sink into my memory so that I could sketch it later.

I shook my head, knowing that a painting of this could never do it justice. The one thing every creator comes to realize is that some things can never be captured. A story, a photograph, or a painting can never encapsulate living beauty to its fullest. I could never paint the smell of croissants when they're fresh out of the oven, add the sound of an infant crying in the distance, or the feel of dampness in the air. Sometimes, an artist realizes they were put in that moment to simply appreciate its beauty and treasure the ability to live within it without trying to reproduce it. This was one of those moments. I gave a small nod of respect as the moment passed, then turned to continue my quiet walk.

I was early for Mass, so I wandered into the church. After saying my morning offering, I let my mind wander until a phrase landed. *Keep your friends close, but your enemies closer.* I immediately thought of Luke. Where did he fall on that spectrum? Friend or enemy? I'd been enjoying my time in France, but I was still waiting to find out the real reason for my being here. Luke said he wanted to be inspired to paint again, but he hadn't seemed interested in being with me while I was sketching. And he barely glanced over my work when I shared it with him the first couple of weeks I was here. I couldn't help but wonder why this talented artist was keeping me around. There was more to this.

These thoughts ran through my mind while I waited for Mass to begin. I knew I should be preparing for the hour ahead, but my mind was adrift. As the church began to fill, I knelt down on the kneeler to try and focus. My medal fell from my V-neck dress and clinked against the pew in front of me. That happened sometimes. I would always touch it, say a quick Hail Mary, and then drop it back into place. But today, I thought of Luke. His comment about the trinket around my neck had been strange, but he had gone white as a ghost when he saw my medal. I had forgotten all about that part. My anger had blocked out the reason he had backed away, right before he called me by the name of his late wife. There was more there, but what? I stewed about that all through Mass. I knew what I needed to do. I had to go visit Anne.

I had been avoiding our meeting. Just like a child who hadn't been obedient, I didn't want Anne to know that I not only didn't stay away from Luke, but I was actually living in the studio behind his house. My Southern upbringing had driven in "respect your elders" to a fault. Still, I knew the day had come.

Anne had shared with me that her husband had bad afternoons, but his mornings were good. So, after Mass let out, I purchased a fresh bouquet of flowers from a street vendor who was just setting up shop for the day, and I made my way back to my grandfather's old neighborhood. Once again, goosebumps popped up as I turned the corner and saw the main street. I could almost picture him walking on these same cobblestones as he walked home from Mass, too. I smiled and made my way to Anne's doorway.

It wasn't quite 8:30, so I knocked quietly, but no one came to the door. I knocked a second time, but still no one answered. A passerby stopped and called out something to me in French.

"English?" I asked.

The older lady rolled her eyes and said, "Church," then turned to move past me.

I knew better. During my time in France, I learned that the French would always be more receptive if you apologized for not knowing their language instead of assuming they know English. Even if, in all actuality, they did. The only thing to do at this point was to thank her, so I called out, "*Merci!*" She only lifted her hand in response. I'll try hard not to make that mistake again.

Remembering the café across the street, I walked over and found a seat at the same table I was at before, which had a great view of Anne's front doorway. I ordered coffee and watched the hustle and bustle of a neighborhood street on a Sunday. Over the course of the next hour, it seemed like every local was on the street. All the businesses were closed except for the restaurants, and people were enjoying themselves. I was so busy people watching that I almost missed Anne and her husband arrive at their doorway.

"Oh my gosh, he looks just like Grandfather Gerard," I heard myself mumble. An unexpected sadness grabbed hold of me. The cry that arose in my throat made the bite of the croissant I had just taken seem to double in size in my mouth. I coughed it into my napkin, then took a sip of water. I had not prepared myself for this. *I have a relative living in France who looks just like my grandfather.* Why hadn't I known about him before? Did my mom know?

I watched as Anne helped him into their home. He was hunched over and feeble, but he still paused to pinch her cheek as she held the door open for him. *He's still got some spunk in him; that's good,* I thought. *They need some time to get settled.* So, I took my time finishing my coffee. It was probably good that I watched them walk up. If I had walked inside their house and met him for the first time face-to-face, I probably would have fainted. At least now, I was a little more prepared.

Chapter 33

A Visit

Anne wasn't surprised to see me. In fact, she seemed to have been expecting me. I wondered if she saw me sitting in the café.

"Janine, welcome. Come in, come in," Anne said, drawing out long syllables in a sing-song way.

Their main doorway was set back from the walkway with decorative iron doors on the streetside. I had been waiting on the landing until she came to the door and was happy to escape the summer's heat. Their house was small with only two windows on the street side, but it was perfect for a small family, or in this case, an aging couple. I walked directly into a living room that was simple but neat. Her husband was sitting in the only single chair in the room. If he had been born in the United States, he would most likely be settled into a comfortable recliner. But in his home, he was in an armchair with wooden legs. Somehow, I felt proud of him, but I had no idea why.

He smiled up as I approached, then addressed me. "*Bonjour*, Janine. Anne told me all about meeting you. I'm very pleased you came for a visit."

"It's nice to meet you, too, Mr...." I suddenly realized I didn't know his name. I stumbled over my words but was saved quickly.

"Call me Robèrt."

He didn't look as much like my grandfather up close. His hair was bushy, as well as his eyebrows, and he had kind eyes that appeared to sparkle, almost as if he were the only one privy to a joke. On the contrary, my grandfather was very serious. His eyes always seemed to be studying me.

Anne interrupted. "We were just sitting down for breakfast; would you please join us?"

I didn't want to intrude and was about to tell them I had already eaten, when my stomach answered with a loud growl. I sighed. "That would be lovely, thank you."

Anne led me into the kitchen to a small round table topped with a periwinkle blue tablecloth. She motioned to the chair for me to sit. I watched as she went about her morning, setting the table where she'd eaten her breakfast for decades. She placed the coffee cups at each place, then put the pot of coffee onto a beautiful silver holder. She placed a small dish with some jam beside a small plate with slices of something that appeared to be cheese.

As soon as Robèrt was seated, she placed his plate in front of him, then set both of ours in place. The meal was modest. Each of our plates held two slices from a crusty baguette, a peeled boiled egg, and a small bowl of plain yogurt. They bowed their heads and said a blessing in French, then began. I watched as they dipped jam onto one of the slices of bread. They topped the other slice with a piece of the thickly cut cheese. I followed their example and did the same. The bread was as hard as a rock. What I thought to be cheese turned out to be the creamiest butter I'd ever tasted. I was eager to see how they ate the egg and was happy when Anne picked it up with her fingers and took a bite off the top. Memories of dying eggs at Easter filled my mind. That was the only day of the year I would usually even think of eating a boiled egg. Still, I followed Anne's direction once again and was pleasantly surprised. My thoughts of Easter's past were suddenly interrupted when Robèrt cleared his throat.

"Janine, Anne tells me you're from the United States, yes?"

"I am. I live in a city named Savannah in the state of Georgia."

"Ah, interesting. And my cousin, Gerard, lived there, also?"

"Yes, that would be my grandfather. He did."

"I tried to track him down many years ago but only got as far as New Orleans."

I smiled. "He told me that's where he was living before the opportunity to work on the cathedral in Savannah became available. That's where he met my grandmother."

"I'm sorry to hear of his passing," Robèrt said, reaching over and patting my hand twice before pulling away.

"Thank you. I miss him terribly," I answered, feeling the familiar sting that death brings.

He continued. "Anne tells me you're an artist. She said you are even more gifted than Gerard."

"My grandfather taught me everything I know," I answered, suddenly very protective of him.

"Ah, did he teach or did he encourage?"

I didn't answer right away. Instead, I took a long sip of my coffee while pondering the question. Finally, I decided to answer the question with a question. "Aren't they the same?"

He smiled knowingly. "No, they're definitely not. A person being taught is shown how to do something. A person being encouraged already knows how, even if it's still a gift that hasn't been opened." I only nodded as I mulled this over in my mind. Anne rose and began to clear the plates, so I scooted my chair out to help. Robèrt reached over and gently set his hand on top of mine, nodding his head to keep me in place. "Now tell me, Janine, what brings you to Montmartre?"

My eyes darted to Anne, who set the plates on the counter and moved quickly back into her seat.

"I recently graduated from art school in Savannah. Luke Depris came to give the commencement address. We spoke afterwards and he asked me to come back to Paris with him."

Robèrt rubbed his hand along the razor stubble on his chin. "You seem like a smart girl. Do you believe it was pure coincidence that you were brought to the very same place where your grandfather was born?"

I've always heard of people having lightning-bolt moments, and this was mine. How could I have been so dumb? I exhaled loudly. "Obviously, I'm not as smart as you think."

"Tell me, Janine. What do you know about your gift?"

"My gift?"

"Yes. The gift passed down in our family."

"Nothing. I've never heard of this."

Robèrt angrily began speaking French rapidly to Anne. She stood, as their conversation went back and forth, referencing me with their hands. Finally, their voices softened. I assumed Anne was the one who lost their conflict when she leaned against the table to address me. "Did your grandfather tell you anything about the Miraculous Medal?"

Reaching inside my shirt, I pulled out my medal. "He gave this to me."

Anne gasped, covering her mouth with her hands, and then she plopped back into her chair. She softly said something to Robèrt in French before turning back to me. "We thought the last person with the gift had died the day that Eliana fell from the cliff. What a blessing you are, for all of us."

The room went silent as they studied me. *They obviously*

believe something that just isn't true. I'm a decent artist, but I know my limits. I'm certainly not a blessing. Besides, I'm fed up with France and ready to go home. No, that's not true. France is lovely. I'm fed up with Luke. But, how can I tell them? They are very sweet, and I don't want to burst their bubble, but they must know. I sat up straight in my chair and belted it out. "I think you got the wrong girl. I really wish I could help you, but I'm not all that and certainly not considered a blessing."

They burst out laughing—side-splitting, slap-your-knee, laughing.

I stood so quickly that my chair screeched. They immediately stopped laughing. "Okay then, I think I'd better hit the road," I blurted out.

"Hit the road?" Robèrt asked.

"Yes, I need to leave. It was nice to meet you. My grandfather was very lucky to have such a nice family. I wish you both well," I said as I moved toward the doorway.

"Wait," Anne called out just as I was almost out of the kitchen. I paused only a second before she was at my side. For an old gal, she sure could get around quickly. She walked in front of me and took my hands into hers. Her motherly warmth soothed my confusion. "I know this is a lot to process. We've known this story our whole life. I can't imagine hearing this for the first time. But will you please educate yourself on this before running from it?" I sighed, then nodded, so she continued. "You should go to the source of the story. The Chapel of Our Lady of the Miraculous Medal. It is located inside the Motherhouse of the Daughters of Charity in Paris. They open their doors every morning at 7:45. Thousands of pilgrims go there daily to visit the apparition site and the remains of Saint Catherine Labouré, but you can go directly to the information desk and ask to speak to Sister Louise. Show her your medal and she will explain everything."

I looked into her eyes as she spoke. She was kind and meant me no harm. Dropping her hands, I moved past her, but something made me pause. Turning, my eyes landed on Robèrt, who at that moment looked so much like my grandfather. "Thank you both," I mumbled. Their worried faces made me sad, so I forced a smile and added, "I'll see you soon."

Chapter 34

Jumping in Puddles

The sun accosted me the moment my feet hit the cobbled sidewalk. It was directly overhead and burned my scalp with its intensity. All the Sunday strollers who had packed the streets when I went inside Anne's home had taken shelter from the midday heat. Those who were left hurried along to their destination.

As I came to the end of the street, I heard children's laughter. It broke through my distress like a beacon of hope. I followed the walkway to a small park that ran between the buildings. The greenspace looked like an oasis amid the hot pavement that surrounded it, but the extraordinary thing was that every sprinkler in the park was running at top capacity.

There were hundreds of children dancing in the spray. The younger ones chased one another, while the older ones just stood underneath to cool off.

As I walked closer, I noticed the adults who were standing on the walkway. They had all kicked their shoes off, too. The run-off from the sprinklers puddled on the pavement, and the teens and young adults stomped in the cool water. I couldn't resist, so I slid my sandals off and did the same. There is something freeing about stomping in water. It reminded me of jumping in puddles as a child. I immediately had the feeling I was doing something I wasn't supposed to and half waited for my parents to reprimand me. There were no rules or boundaries, just simple fun.

I glanced around at my fellow splashers of all ages, but my gaze landed on someone on the side taking pictures. It gave me pause when I realized the camera was pointed right at me. The photographer slowly lowered the camera from his face and nodded at me before returning it to his eye and aiming at a new subject. The thought of someone actually catching all this joy in a photo made me happy, especially since it was a spontaneous moment in Parisian life.

After a few minutes, the sprinklers stopped. Both children and adults moaned in unison with disappointment. The fun was now over. The children went in search of their parents, and the adults went in search of their shoes. I found a bench to sit on and began to buckle my sandals when I heard the click of the camera. I eyed him suspiciously and was surprised when he walked toward me.

He began to speak quickly in French. I shook my head and carefully apologized, then asked if he spoke English. "*Désolé, parlez-vous anglais?*"

"Ah, an American. Okay, I was apologizing for making you uncomfortable, but let's just say you're easy to photograph. Your face shows great emotion, and you don't try to hide it. It's a gift."

I was about to tell him thank you, but then he continued to speak. "And...you don't see many women stomping in puddles in their Sunday dresses. You Americans are very interesting."

"Uh, thank you?" I responded, then picked up my bag to leave.

He seemed amused, either by my confusion or by the possibility I would walk away from a handsome French photographer. "I'm Joseph," he threw out.

I knew who he was. I had been briefly introduced to him at the gallery. "I'm Jan. I actually saw your exhibit at the gallery. You have a great eye."

He didn't answer immediately. Instead, he tilted his head as if he were trying to recall our meeting. His face changed when it registered. "Ah! You're the artist staying with Luke. I thought you looked familiar. You were the one feeding Luke his signals at the interview."

He said it in passing, but it embarrassed me. I could only imagine how crazy I looked with my hands flying in every direction, trying to help that egotistical man answer the interviewer's questions. I finally answered, "Guilty!"

"Yes, yes. I've heard a lot about you. Luke has never taken an intern before. We are all very interested."

"We?"

"Yes. There is a group of us that works with the studio. We offer classes, give talks, and do whatever we can do to make ends meet while doing what we love. Montmartre has many artists in our community—it always has."

"I know. It's crazy. I'm walking the same streets as the greats. You must stay inspired every day."

He paused once again. Thankfully, this time it was brief. "Why don't you come and meet the group?" He must have sensed my reservations, because he quickly added, "There are only six of us and we love all creatives."

I answered before thinking it through. "I'd love to; when do you meet?"

"I'm on my way there now."

I looked down at my still-damp dress and dirty feet, and said, "I'm not going to be able to come today. Sorry."

"You look fine. It's casual. Come on." He picked up my bag from the bench and began to walk away. I stepped quickly behind him to catch up. He glanced my way and nodded with a smile. We walked quietly as we exited the park, then he asked what I was doing on the other side of Montmartre.

"I was visiting some family," I answered truthfully.

"Very nice; what are their names?"

"Anne and Robèrt Gereau," I answered.

Joseph stopped walking and turned to face me. "You're related to Robèrt Gereau? He's a legend. Almost every piece of metalwork you see in Montmartre was made by him. I photograph his decorative iron fences often. Could you introduce me?"

"I'm not sure if I'll see him again before I leave."

"Leave? Why are you leaving? You landed the position to be Luke's intern. Surely you know how special that is, don't you? You get to work alongside the most famous artist of our time."

I stifled a laugh before answering. "Yes, I am very lucky."

"So, you'll stay. And when you do, you can introduce me to Robèrt Gereau," he uttered, sounding like he had just solved all the problems of the world. Then, he turned and continued walking. I matched his pace and walked beside him as he pointed out places he thought I might be interested in visiting. "That shop has the best macarons; This is a great place to pick up art supplies; That's where Picasso had an art studio." After several blocks, he walked into the open door of a glass-front establishment with the words "Café – Bar" running boldly across the length of the building. He waved to the man behind the bar, who was mixing a drink. The man looked over his metal-rimmed glasses and nodded towards the back of the bar. We walked down a small hallway that emptied into a large room where a group of three males and two females were sitting. They excitedly welcomed Joseph to the table. He walked to the open chair, but instead of sitting, he leaned over to the girl already seated beside him and kissed her. The kiss continued so long that the others at the table lost interest and turned to me.

"*Bonjour*," I announced with my best French sing-song inflections. I must have hit it perfectly because the group began to introduce themselves in French. Thankfully, the love encounter between Joseph and the long-haired brunette ended and he piped in, explaining who I was. I wasn't exactly sure what he said, but I heard Luke's name and Robèrt's.

The table went quiet as they studied me, then one by one they introduced themselves in English. One of the men retrieved a chair for me and slid it on the other side of Joseph, then they all began to ask me questions. Each question built off the previous one. Each one dived a little deeper as they got to know me. Somewhere, about five questions in, a drink was set in front of me as I shared with them my background, my art, my family, and finally my internship with Luke.

"Have you seen his new masterpiece?" the stocky young man asked while tapping the ash of his cigarette onto the floor. I'd seen him before, but where?

The group was surprised by the news of a new painting. They obviously hadn't been privy to the same information. He looked around the table. "What? Didn't you know? He's been working on a new piece day and night and it's almost complete." The plump friend smiled, clearly pleased to have known something the others hadn't. He took a long drag of his cigarette before sitting back in his chair. He smirked before turning to me to respond.

It hit me when I saw that smirk. He was the young man whispering in the doorway with Renae at Luke's interview at the gallery. They seemed to be as close as thieves. I didn't trust him one bit. Still, all eyes were on me, so I was forced to answer. "I have not seen his new art piece, but if Luke painted it, then it must be another masterpiece," I replied. My words, "If he painted it," echoed in my head. I hoped they didn't pick up on my choice of the word "if". But more than anything, I hoped my suspicions were incorrect.

Chapter 35

The Potters

I thought about the group on my walk home, playing back each of their faces around the table. Both girls seemed nice. The petite blonde, Kara, asked me to come to her pottery class tonight. The brunette, Sophie, asked me to come back to their next group meeting. It felt good to be included, especially by fellow artists, although I was still not sure what type of artist each one was. Kara was obviously a ceramist, and Joseph a photographer, but I never asked about the others. They had so many questions for me that I didn't get a chance to ask about them. Thankfully, Sophie said they meet every Monday and Thursday at three, so I should have plenty of time to find out more about each of them.

A tingle of excitement ran through me at the thought of being with them again. The energy of sitting with them reminded me of being with the tribe—minus the sneaky French they said quietly to one another. There was always something to discuss with my friends, someone who needed advice, and a power that came with the knowledge of being loved and supported by others. My friends really are the best.

I walked slowly, enjoying the shade of the side streets from the tall buildings on each side. The afternoon sun was still hot, but at least it wasn't directly overhead. I was thankful I was acclimated to warmer weather. Southerners joke about having thin blood, which gives us the ability to withstand heat better than our Northern neighbors. I know it's just a saying, but it's interesting to consider how our bodies adapt to the temperature we're accustomed to. Still, I got excited when the studio came into view, knowing I would be out of the heat soon. My dress had become stiff after drying from the sprinklers. All I wanted to do was throw it off and jump between the cool white sheets of my bed, but when I opened my main door, I realized I had a guest.

"Jorge," I yelled out with excitement. Although I had only met him briefly when I first arrived, I had been praying for his quick recovery.

Jorge had been straightening my kitchen area and restocking the staple items I had used. He jumped when he heard his name. Turning, he smiled when he saw me in the doorway. "*Bonjour, Mademoiselle* Janine."

I smiled and did some form of a curtsy, although I have no idea why. "How are you?"

"Much better. I understand you are the person who saved me by calling for help. Thank you."

"You're very welcome," I answered, then was at a complete loss for words. I glanced down at the floor, and he turned back to the shelves in the kitchen. "You don't have to do anything in here. I can take care of myself," I added. He turned to me with a small but kind smirk, then looked around the small studio. My eyes followed his stare. The bed was unmade, there was a towel thrown across the back of a metal chair, and apparently, I'd eaten all the staples.

Smiling, he said, "I'm sorry I left you when you had only

just arrived. I look forward to seeing much more of you." Walking toward the door, he added. "Oh, the reason that I came by was to inform you that Mr. Depris is away, but when he returns tomorrow, he would like to take you to dinner. The reservation is for eight."

"Thank you," I whispered as I held the door open for him. I didn't want to admit that I hadn't even noticed he was gone. Truth be known, I had gotten accustomed to being alone.

As Jorge went through, he paused, then turned back. "And, *Mademoiselle*, I think it would be wise to lock your door when you leave. You never know who could just walk right in."

I thanked him one more time and slowly closed the door behind him. My thoughts jumped to the night before. I wasn't worried about the people on the outside who could walk in; it was the ghost that lived inside.

————

JORGE MEANDERED DOWN THE PATH BACK TO THE HOUSE, his mind tumbling with worry. When Luke had visited him in the hospital, he said he was painting and working on a big project that Renae had approved. But Jorge had checked every room of the house and hadn't seen any artwork painted by Luke. The only paintings in the house were sitting in Jan's small studio, which he had just left, and Luke was definitely not the artist.

A sick feeling came over him. *They must be moving forward with their evil scheme of employing Jan to paint in Eliana's place. But why would Luke lie to him? Surely Luke's new project was at his gallery,* he thought. He had to get inside the studio to see for himself. Knowing that Luke was out of town for the evening, he decided to go to the gallery. Every week-night, they hosted a lecture or a class that always began at seven o'clock. Tonight, he would be a participant. It would give him the perfect opportunity to look around.

Jorge knew the classes filled up quickly, so he arrived early to make sure he got a space. He approached the receptionist and told her he'd like to register for the class. She eyed him up and down, then asked, "Are you sure? You may be a little over-dressed."

He looked down at his dark suit that he always wore to work. "It's fine. I'll take off the jacket."

"Whatever you say, sir," she said as she rang up his purchase.

Jorge began to worry, so he asked, "Is this a lecture or a class tonight?"

The receptionist giggled. "Uh, it's a pottery class."

"Pottery?"

"Yes, sir. And the instructor is amazing. You'll love it."

"Doubt it," he mumbled as he walked inside.

He was instructed to don an apron, grab a block of clay, and find an empty wheel. Begrudgingly, he complied. He took off his jacket and then his vest and grabbed a tan apron. He cringed when he saw the mound of mud, knowing his white shirt would be covered in the chocolate brown color soon. He rolled up the sleeves of his white dress shirt as far as he could before cutting himself out a block of the clay, then he searched the room for an empty wheel. There was one in the front, directly in front of the teacher, and one in the back right of the room. He chose the one in the back. He sat down and plopped his mud in the center of the wheel. His muddied hands hung awkwardly in the air, almost like a surgeon who had just been prepped for a procedure. He was out of his element and extremely uncomfortable. Then, out of nowhere, a piece of mud was flung at him. He turned angrily to the person next to him, ready to explode, but instead was met by Jan's kind face, smiling broadly. Relief washed over him as he pinched off a small piece and carefully tossed it back in her direction.

"I'm so happy to see you," Jan admitted. "I was getting nervous doing this alone."

He leaned over, whispering quietly, "These poor students have no idea of the masterpieces we'll be creating tonight; this is going to be fun."

They quieted when Kara began the class. She explained, "This is a beginner pottery class. Today, you'll learn how to get your clay ready, how to use the wheel, and how to make a small bowl. The main focus is on how to feel comfortable on the potter's wheel. They have been used for thousands of years, so don't be intimidated by them. Just find your groove and have fun."

The class followed along, but as soon as everyone's wheels began to spin, Jorge excused himself to go to the restroom. Wiping his hands on his apron, he went out into the hallway, but he kept walking past the bathroom and towards the studio. He knew his way around; he had come so often with Luke. He searched each room but found nothing that even closely resembled something Luke would have painted. When he turned to leave the last room, the young artist named Sophie was standing in the doorway.

"Hey, I recognize you. You work for Luke."

He cringed. "Yes, I do," he answered. He had been caught snooping.

"This is the room where I'm having my showing next week. Were you looking for me?" Sophie asked.

He had to think quickly. Why would he be back here covered in clay? "No. I was in a class and took a break to run to the restroom. I remembered Luke telling me I needed to check out your work before your showing." He paused, wondering if she was buying it.

Her eyes brightened with excitement. "Luke said that about me? Wow, I'm honored. So, what do you think?"

"Brilliant," he answered. She smiled, so he added, "I know you'll have a great show."

"I sure hope so. I'm happy he let me have my showing before he unveils his next work."

Jorge pondered her statement. He needed to know more. "I've been in the hospital and haven't been able to see the painting yet. Is it here at the studio?"

"No," she answered. "I heard about it from a friend just today. I'm dying to see it, so I searched the studio earlier, but it's not here. I bet he's keeping it at his home studio for now. It's all very exciting."

Jorge smiled. "Yes, it is. Very exciting." Turning to leave, he added, "It was really nice to see you again. Good luck." He walked slowly down the hall, pondering the information he had just been told. Why in the world would Luke tell people about a piece of art that didn't exist? No, why would he lie to him? Jorge was so deep in thought that when he turned the corner to go back to the classrooms, he ran right into Jan.

"Hey. We're taking a break. Are you all right?"

He looked her over. Her oversized apron hung down past her shorts, making it appear that she wasn't wearing anything underneath. She was cute. But more than that, she was a genuine person. "I'm fine. I just haven't regained my strength from the hospital. I think I'm going to head home. Could you please put my clay away?"

"I can, but why don't I come with you instead. You shouldn't be walking alone if you don't feel well."

"I'll be fine, but thanks," he answered and took a couple of steps towards the door. He sensed her watching him. He turned to find her face weighted with worry. "Jan, can I ask you something?"

"Sure, anything."

"Have you seen Luke painting anything recently?

She smirked. "You're the second person who's asked me that today. No, I have never seen him paint. Not one thing since I've been here. That's odd, isn't it?"

Jorge nodded. "I would say it is definitely odd if a painter doesn't paint," he answered with a smile. She began to walk away, but he asked, "Oh, and who was the other person who asked?"

"One of the artists who works here," Jan answered. "All of the artists are really excited about the news of his new work and can't wait to see it."

They were interrupted when Kara walked into the hall and announced that class was about to reconvene, so Jan said, "I guess I'd better get back. The wheel waits for no one. Bye, Jorge."

Jorge watched her leave. If his intuition was right, Luke and Renae were about to either buy or steal one of her beautiful paintings. Jorge's thoughts jumped to Renae. And suddenly, he remembered their fight in the driveway. She had watched him carry Luke's paintings to the incinerator. All except one. She had followed him into the back room, where Jorge had saved some of Luke's prettiest paintings. Luke was still a very talented artist, even if he wasn't recognized for his own art. Renae had approached him just as he locked up the room, demanding to get inside to destroy all his work. He had told Renae no. That's when he began to back away from her ranting and tripped.

His hand instinctively jumped to the large scar on his head. *She's dangerous*, he thought, not for the first time. Jan deserved better, and Jorge was going to help her, even if it cost him the loss of his best friend.

Chapter 36

Daughters of Charity

The cool air hit my face the moment I stepped out of the studio. I had enjoyed working with the clay, and the artist in me always loves to create, but tonight my mind was elsewhere. After Jorge left the studio, I tried to push our brief conversation out of my mind. He was worried; it showed all over his face.

Like me, Jorge was trying to piece things together. Maybe I should have said more. Maybe I should have confided in him. But Jorge was Luke's best friend. There's no way he would have believed me over Luke.

I needed answers, especially after the conversation I had with Anne and Robèrt. Instinctively, I reached up and touched the medal swinging around my neck. It had fallen loose while I was leaning over the potter's wheel and now was free and exposed. *How many times do I touch this medal a day without realizing it?* I only took it off to shower, but I rarely looked at it closely. Anne had explained it briefly, but surely there was more to the story. I decided I'd go to the chapel tomorrow and find out.

I woke up early the following morning, walked to the Abbesses Station, and took Metro Line 12 into the city. When I got off, I made my way to the motherhouse of the Daughters of Charity and went to the Chapel of Our Lady of the Miraculous Medal. I remembered that Anne told me to go directly to the information desk, so I did. The line of people who needed information was long, but I waited my turn until I was finally met in the front by a very plump and very French nun.

"May I please speak to Sister Louise?" I asked.

She pointed to herself and shook her head no, so I repeated, "Sister Louise, please." She said three quick words I didn't understand, then leaned to address the person behind me. The next person came beside me and began to speak to the buxom sister. I didn't move an inch, yet they spoke as if I wasn't there at all. I held up my hand in front of their face to stop their conversation. This infuriated the nun, who then slammed her hand down on her desk and began to give me a proper scolding in French.

Well, this ain't my first rodeo, Sister. I grew up in Catholic schools. So, I closed my eyes, made the Sign of the Cross, and held up my best praying hands. The yelling stopped. I waited a second, then peeked out of one of my closed eyes to find that the angry, chubby nun had been replaced by a much older and slimmer one. The good sister had her arms crossed and showed no emotion. This one meant business. Her stern face made my hands drop by my side.

"How can I help you?" she asked in perfect English.

I stood tall and answered, "Good morning, Sister. May I please speak to Sister Louise?"

"I'm Sister Louise," she replied.

I dug the chain from the inside of my shirt and showed her the medal that hung from it. Her eyes widened. She reached out to me and took both my hands into hers. "How did you come by this?" she asked.

"It was my grandfather's," I answered.

She patted my hand before announcing, "We must talk. Follow me."

I felt the plump nun's glare. I shrugged and stuck out my tongue as her face turned crimson, then I followed Sister Louise. We cut through the open corridor, passing the gift shop and the chapel. She turned into a private doorway that appeared to be the Daughters of Charity residence. When we reached the end of the hallway, we turned into her office. She motioned me to a chair before walking around the desk and sitting down herself. Once we were sitting face-to-face, she smiled. "Can I please see the medal again?" she asked.

I took the necklace from around my neck and set it on the desk. Her hands trembled as she picked it up, studying it in detail. Pulling a magnifying glass from her desk, she turned it from the front to the back before saying, "It's amazing. Truly amazing."

I felt guilty for not knowing its importance. But this is why I came here—to get answers. I mustered up my courage and asked, "Could you please tell me about this medal I wear? I understand it is special, but I'm not sure why." I watched her face glaze over in confusion.

"You don't know the story of the medal?"

"I know from school that Saint Catherine of Labouré had a vision of the Virgin Mary, who instructed her to have medals with her image made, and that some of the people who wore them were granted miraculous healings," I answered.

"Yes, the Virgin Mary instructed Saint Catherine of Labouré to have the medal designed with the image of Mary the Immaculata. It shows rays of light from the hands of the Virgin, who is gazing downward as if listening to the pleas of the devout. After a long inquiry, the task to make these medals was given to Adrien-Jean-Maximilien Vachette, one of the official jewelers of Louis XVIII's court. He produced two thousand medals in the 1830s.

The Daughters of Charity began wearing them and giving them to the elderly and sick. Almost immediately, miraculous healings, cures, and conversions occurred; people began clamoring for the Medal of the Immaculate Conception, as it was originally called. The medal quickly spread throughout France and then the world. Before long, people were calling it the Miraculous Medal; everyone wanted the medal that Mary had brought from Heaven. Not only did the Archbishop of Paris request some of the first medals, but Pope Gregory XVI also put one at the foot of the crucifix on his desk.

When the terrible cholera epidemic broke out, the medals were in such high demand that they needed other goldsmiths to help produce more. That's where your story comes in. One of the goldsmiths was part of your family in Montmartre. I'm not sure of the other families, but it is said that your ancestor asked to meet with Saint Catherine of Labouré and she was so impressed by his willingness and humbleness that she asked him to craft a special medal to be passed down in just his family to recognize the special artists in the family. I truly thought the last one had been buried with its owner a few years ago.

My mind was spinning. There was another artist with this same medal who died a few years ago? My stomach tightened. I didn't want to know but knew that I must ask. Clearing my throat, I inquired, "Since it would be my family, could you please share with me the name of the artist who passed away?"

Sister Louise's face showed her emotions. She was uneasy but eventually agreed. "Her last name had been Laroche, but she had married. What was her new name?" Sister Louise's sharp memory came into focus. "Depris. Eliana Depris."

I felt the blood leave my head as a cold chill ran down my spine. I could barely make out what Sister Louise was saying as she casually continued our conversation. Her voice seemed to be underwater. She stood and walked out of the room, while my mind continued reeling. By the time she returned with tea and pastries, I had steadied myself. She asked about my personal life, where I was from, and if I happened to be an artist. Then she asked me if I'd like to see my family's file.

The folder was stuffed with early drawings. There were black-and-white photos that transitioned into various forms of colored ones, and more recently, an obituary. I studied each one intently while Sister Louise sipped her tea, then I closed the file when I was done.

"Do you have any questions for me?" she asked.

I felt numb. *Questions. Do I have questions?* I heard myself answer, "No, Sister. Thank you so much for sharing all of this with me." When she stood, I followed, and we walked back out the way we came. As we reached the information desk, she told me I was always welcome. Then, she stopped walking and turned me slowly until we were face-to-face. She placed each of her hands on my shoulders and said, "Stay safe and guard both the medal and your art. I'll keep you in my prayers."

Chapter 37

Grieving

I found my way back to the station, and once I was settled back on the Metro Line 12 train, I let myself go to the place I wouldn't—until now. Had Eliana painted all of Luke's famous paintings? And, if so, had Luke killed her for them? *Is that even possible?* The warnings from Anne and Robèrt filled my mind, followed by the words Sister Louise said at our parting, "Guard your medal and your art."

I stared out the window at the perpetual darkness of the underground metro line. Closing my eyes, I thought about the many conversations with people about Luke's art. Everyone told me how lucky I was to be studying under such a great artist and how much I was surely learning by watching him paint. But I'd been in Paris for weeks now and not once had I seen his skills. Did he paint at all? Yes. Or at least he did. I'd seen proof when I walked around his study in Avignon, viewing the many pictures hanging on the wall. Shaking my head, I knew I had my answer. Luke had definitely taken Eliana's paintings and called them his own.

The train moved along, stopping every five minutes or so at

the various stations, then speeding off as fast as it came in. My anxiety level grew, as the train drew closer to Montmartre. *Am I in danger?* If Luke had killed his wife for her paintings, would he kill again? Lights flashed in various points in the tunnel as I stared out the window, trying to calm my nerves. The next thing I saw was the doors closing as the train pulled away from the Abbesses Station. I missed my stop. I'd get off at the next one and walk the short distance back.

A few minutes later, I departed at a station by the name of Lamarck. I climbed the stairs and exited onto a busy, yet charming, neighborhood street in the northern section of Montmartre. People were photographing themselves in front of the metro station sign, so I stopped to take notice. I remembered Joseph talking about Robèrt's intricate metal work surrounding the red and green metro station signs in Montmartre, and this one was striking. He truly was a talented artist.

Being outside seemed to calm my nerves, so I decided to take my time walking back and enjoy this section of Montmartre. Thankfully, I had a good sense of direction. Just like in Savannah, if you knew which direction the cathedral was, you could find your way. I searched for my bearings. I knew how to get to Sacre Coeur from here, and once I was there, I could find my way home from there. So, I decided to relax and wander about for a while.

I followed a cute couple with two small children into the Square Suzanne Buisso. When they turned toward the playground, I wandered over to the statue of Saint Denis holding his head in his hands. I'd never get used to seeing a headless statue, but something about it was intriguing. When I was a little girl, my parents would sometimes take my sister and me to Savannah's downtown cathedral for Mass instead of our local parish. I would crane my neck through the service, staring at the paintings of various saints that ran along the top of the nave.

The one that I focused on every time was Saint Denis. Standing in front of this statue, I was still in awe. As I turned to leave the headless saint, a child's laughter caught my attention. That's when I saw him. Or at least, I thought it was him. But this man looked odd walking across the park, almost as if he was wandering or his mind was somewhere else. I decided to follow him to find out for sure. He trotted down the steps and followed the path around the park's side until it turned into the sidewalk on the street. I followed, skirting around the neighborhood people, who were going about their normal, everyday lives.

I followed closely, but not too closely. When he stopped at a flower shop, I slid behind a rack of postcards at a neighborhood store, flipping through them one by one. From this vantage point, I confirmed it was Luke. The owner called out his name and held up his order. With flowers in hand, he continued his walk until he entered the Montmartre Cemetery. I hid behind a large domed crypt as he walked down the stairs to a lower level, then continued down along the cobbled path. The area was small and confined, so I watched, but didn't move from my hiding place.

Luke stopped in front of a grave and sat on the ground. "Wow!" I mumbled. I didn't expect that. He fiddled with the grass around him as he talked. I was so far away, I couldn't hear him. And to be honest, it was such a private moment, I didn't want to. I almost turned away, not wanting to intrude, but then he became animated, laughing and using his hands to express himself. I couldn't pull my eyes away. I was surprised when he hopped up. He moved quickly. He leaned over the tombstone to an attached metal vase on its base. Removing an older bouquet that was brown and rotting, he replaced it with his bright new bunch.

As Luke began to walk my way, I realized I was trapped. I

squatted down as low as I could, praying my backside wasn't sticking out. The sound of his steps grew closer. I could smell his cologne. He really needed to tone his liberal amount down. But as it faded, so did the sound of his steps. I peeked my head from around my shelter as he disappeared behind the cemetery's gate. Exhaling loudly, I struggled to rise, then I began to walk toward the grave he had just visited. I noticed a groundskeeper nearby, so I asked, "Was that Luke Depris?"

He smiled. "Ah. An American fan. *Oui.* That was Mr. Depris. He comes here weekly."

I thanked him and continued to the gravesite. The area was boxed off by an iron coping, keeping the graves inside separated from the rest of its landowners. An intricate iron sign, resembling the one from the metro, stood high in the back. It read Montigny. Every tombstone looked identical to my grandfather's in Savannah. They each had the etched figure that was identical to the one hanging around my neck—the Miraculous Medal. I already knew what name would be carved on the most recent grave in the section, the one with the fresh flowers—it was Eliana.

Chapter 38

Confrontation

Jorge stood outside of Luke's room with dread. *Surely, there must be a reasonable explanation for why Luke has been lying to me,* he thought, while knowing in his heart that there was never a good reason to lie. He raised his hand to knock but paused. *Once I confront him, I can't go back. I could lose my job, and more so, I could lose my best friend.* Then he came to his senses. *What kind of friend would I be if I didn't confront him? If I didn't try to save him from making a big mistake?* He knocked twice and entered.

"Oh, thank goodness you're here, my friend. Could you help me with this tie? I just can't get it right tonight," Luke said in frustration.

Jorge came to stand in front of Luke. He waited a split second, searching his eyes for answers. Luke's brow furrowed, so Jorge quickly grabbed both hanging sides of Luke's silk tie and began wrapping it into the perfect knot.

"Is something on your mind, Jorge?" Luke asked.

Jorge remained quiet until he had finished his task at hand.

He straightened Luke's collar and placed his hand on Luke's shoulder before asking, "Can you tell me where you're keeping your new art piece?"

Luke took two steps back. Glancing down at his tie, he began to fiddle with tucking the bottom piece safely under the top. "It's at the gallery," he answered.

Jorge moved closer, not taking his eyes off Luke. "No. It's not. When I couldn't find it anywhere in this house, I went to the gallery. It's not there, either."

Luke turned and crossed the room to his dresser. He began to put on his watch but wasn't able to connect the lock. "You must have missed it. I have it in the back."

Jorge walked up behind him and reached for his wrist. As he closed the catch on the watch, he responded. "I did not miss it because it doesn't exist. You haven't painted a new project."

Luke jumped back. "What? Of course I have. How would you even know? You just came back to work yesterday."

"I know because I know you. I know where your other paintings came from. And I know Renae. She would never let you create your own painting. So, tell me, my friend, what's going on? Maybe I can help."

Luke plopped into an armchair beside the window. Leaning onto one of the arms, he let his head fall into his hand. "I don't think even you can help me out of this one," he said.

"Try me," Jorge encouraged.

Luke sat for a moment, then looked up. "As you know, we've used all of Eliana's paintings. They're all gone. And now it's time to release a new one. Renae sent me to the States to find Jan. I saw her work and really didn't think it would work. I mean, she was good, but nowhere near Eliana. But when she came to Paris and started painting Montmartre, her greatness came alive. Renae snuck into her studio one afternoon and saw one of her extraordinary paintings, and she wants us to release it. She is pressuring me to try and buy Jan off, but my plan is to try and include Jan, to offer her a long-term position painting and pay her a lot of money to do it. Any young artist should be happy to partner with me." Leaning up in his chair, he added, "Jorge, you need to see this painting. It would be a beautiful addition to my work."

"Do you even hear yourself, Luke?" Jorge asked, sitting down in the matching armchair on the other side of the window. "Your work? Renae has brainwashed you."

"I don't know what you mean."

"You have lived this lie for so long, you somehow believe that it's true. Let me take you back to the week when Renae showed Eliana's art as your own. Think hard. Have you forgotten? You were angry, but more than that, you were sad that the world never knew Eliana as you did—as one of the most beautiful painters in the world."

Luke looked stunned but not convinced. Shaking his head, he whispered, "It's not like that?"

"Oh, it's not? Then tell me how it's different?"

"It will be a partnership with Jan."

"Oh, a partnership. Is that how partners work, claiming someone else's art as their own?"

Luke stood abruptly. "Careful, my friend. You're crossing a line here."

Jorge laughed. "I'm crossing a line? Okay. Maybe that's how you see it. But I see it as not wanting my best friend to make the same mistake twice."

Luke sat back down, appearing to be defeated. His voice was barely audible when he spoke. "I don't see another way out of this; what else can I do?"

"You could try telling the truth. You are a great man. You

are a great painter. And you're a hell of a supporter of other artists. People might be angry, but eventually they will see that you're the same old Luke underneath it all."

Luke shook his head. "I hear you, but I'd still like to try with Jan. If she has any reservations or says no, then it's over. I'll come clean."

Jorge slowly shook his head. "And what about Renae? She's not going to let you off that easily."

"Well, that's not really up to her, is it?" Luke answered.

———

CHRISTINE SAT AT THE LARGE KITCHEN TABLE WITH Luke's planner open. She busily filled in all his appointments while the household staff moved around her like she was invisible. She had become such a constant presence that they spoke freely around her. Christine listened to everything but never commented. Part of the job as a personal assistant was to be in the know, and she definitely had that job covered. She knew more about each of them than she ever wanted to know. But her ears perked up when she heard the cook talking about the moonlight desserts planned for Jan and Luke that evening.

"He's taking the American to dinner, then wants desserts and champagne ready to be served at eleven at the table at the cliff's edge," the chef had told her friend.

This is it, Christine thought. Renae had shared the plan to ask Jan if they could buy her painting. Christine knew in her heart that Jan would turn Luke down and worried about what Renae would do if that happened. She had told Christine she would obtain that painting, one way or another, just like she had Eliana's. Christine knew she couldn't let that happen.

She liked Jan. No, more than that, she admired her as an

artist. Jan had approached her several times to go to dinner or to a nightclub for fun, but Christine had turned her down. She had to keep her distance, for her Renae's sake. But tonight, she would take a stand. She would watch from the backyard, and when Luke and Jan were busy, she would take the painting herself and beat Renae to the punch.

Chapter 39

Date With a Narcissist

I tried to cool down by opening the bathroom door. The steam escaped quickly, but the room remained hot. I do some of my best thinking in the shower while letting the scalding water run over my head. Judging from the clouded room, I had too much on my mind. After wiping the fogged bathroom mirror with my towel, I began to brush my wet hair, but I was too hot to think. Maybe if I sat down for a second, I would cool off. So, I walked to the small vanity and sat in the chair.

Cool air ran across my toes. It was so cold that it made me shiver. *What is that and where is it coming from?* I searched the base of the walls for floor vents but didn't see any, so I dropped to my hands and knees and moved in its direction. If there was cold air nearby, I wanted it on my face. The breeze stopped at the linen closet, but it was strong enough at that point that it cooled me down. I leaned on the door jamb until I could think clearly, then rose to get ready for my date.

My date. Isn't that a farce? I can't imagine talking with him for a minute, never mind a couple of hours. Why in the world would he want to go on a date with me anyway? He has been avoiding me for weeks. I was nervous to be around him. Maybe I just knew too much. A small part of me wished I didn't. It was easier when I was just naïve Jan from Georgia, fangirling over the famous artist. But now I knew more about myself, too. I was from a long line of artists from right here in Montmartre. Knowing that gave me strength and it also made me protective of our gift. *He's the one who should be nervous.* Now, I just had to believe everything that I was thinking.

Standing in front of the mirror, I tried for the second time to put mascara on my eyelashes. The first time ended with two black eyes. I had been too distracted, playing back my conversations with both Anne and Sister Louise. I leaned into the mirror, trying hard to steady my hand until I finished. "Good enough," I told myself, knowing that sometimes that's as good as you can get.

Walking back into the main room, a nagging feeling came over me, almost as if someone was whispering it in my ear. "What are the odds you would come straight to Montmartre on your own?" I stopped and let my eyes search the room. Nothing was off, but my mind replayed the question. *What are the odds?* "Zero!" I said into the empty room. *Then who is behind my being here?* Renae's face popped into my mind. I would find her tomorrow and confront her. But that left Luke. Where did he fall in all of this?

The knock came almost as a response. *It's time to stay focused,* I told myself. *I can do this.*

I opened the door for Luke. He was cleanly shaven, tanned, well-dressed in a coat and tie, and smelled great. *Damn him for being so nice looking tonight,* I thought before my mind took control and added, *Too bad he's such a prick.*

He leaned in and kissed both of my cheeks, causing major

butterflies in my stomach. *Traitors!* I thought. Didn't they know I clearly disliked this person?

"You look lovely, my dear," he whispered in my ear. "Are you ready?"

I offered a small grin and nodded, so he offered me his elbow. As I pulled the door shut behind me, I thought of Jorge's warning to lock my door. "Wait just one second. I need to grab my key," I said, then locked the door behind me.

As Luke and I walked into the courtyard, he said, "I made reservations at two different places—Jules Verne, which is inside the Eiffel Tower, and Victor's, where we ate when you first arrived in Paris. You choose."

"All right," I answered. "I choose Victor's."

He smiled broadly. "*Perfecto.* The car is waiting."

We were dropped at the opposite end of the restaurant's walkway this time and had to walk up the narrow path. Once again, it was lined with candles as we drew closer. But when we arrived, the restaurant was empty.

"Where is everybody?" I asked.

"I reserved the whole restaurant tonight," he answered.

I felt my face redden when I noticed the center table was the only one that was dressed. On it sat a bottle of Champagne propped up nicely in a silver bucket of ice. Then I saw the waiting staff standing against the red-bricked wall. They were all there for us. How embarrassing. I nervously began to wring my hands, but as soon as I noticed, I stopped.

Obviously, I didn't stop quickly enough because Luke had noticed, too. He leaned over and said, "Just act like we're here alone. It's not a big deal."

Little did he know that being alone with him unnerved me more than having seven waiters. We sat and began to sip the Champagne.

"Are you enjoying Paris?" he asked.

"Very much so. Not only its beauty, but also its history," I answered.

"Good. Good," he replied, not adding anything further.

When the first course was delivered, we ate in silence. Luke appeared to have something on his mind. As he finished his last bite, he asked, "What are your plans with your Montmartre painting?"

"My plans? I haven't thought it through completely, but I was kind of thinking I would hang it in my Savannah apartment as a memento from my time in France."

Luke seemed surprised, so I quickly turned the conversation to him. "Speaking of paintings, I heard you have a new one coming out."

"Who told you that?" he snipped.

The mood had changed quickly. I could feel it in the air around us. I was reminded of our encounter in Avignon. I sat silently and was relieved that our next course arrived. Once again, we began to eat, but he didn't back down. In a calmer response, he said, "Tell me again who told you I had a new painting coming out?"

I answered, "A guy from your artists' group."

"My artists' group?"

"Yes. The one from your gallery."

"Oh. And how did you get involved with them?"

"I met Joseph, the photographer, and he asked me to meet the group at lunch."

Luke seemed agitated as he took a bite of food, then continued what now felt like an interrogation. "How did you meet Joseph?"

"I was playing in the sprinklers at the park and he was there taking photos."

"And you just started randomly talking?"

I laughed. "Well, it really wasn't random. He recognized me from your interview that day at the gallery. So, as he was leaving the park, he invited me to the artists' group. I was excited to meet your artists. It's really special what you do for local talent."

Luke appeared to relax a bit. "Thank you. We have a great community. And remind me, who said I had a new painting coming out?"

"It was a heavier-set young man who said you were getting ready to unveil a beautiful masterpiece," I replied. "And he seemed happy to deliver the news to the others."

The waiters cleared the entree dishes while my statement hung in the air. Luke stood. "We will have dessert overlooking Paris."

"Oh. We're standing. Okay." I took one last sip of the Champagne, dabbed my lips, then gathered my purse. I matched his stare as I stood and replied, "That sounds delightful." I waved to Victor, who was busy in the kitchen, and blew him a kiss while mouthing "Thank you," then followed Luke outside. It felt wonderful to be in the fresh air; I breathed it in deeply.

We walked back to the house in silence, both lost in our own thoughts. My evening strolls in Montmartre had become one of my favorite times of the day. It was not necessary to converse. The beauty around us was enough. I was surprised to see the house come into view so quickly.

I broke the silence by saying, "Dinner was lovely. Thank you."

"You're welcome," he answered. "And I saved the best for last."

As we turned the corner, he began walking toward the cliff's edge. I was suddenly gripped with fear as thoughts of

Eliana's death flew into my mind. Slowing my walk, I began to come up with reasons to get out of dessert. But as we drew closer, I could see the kitchen staff. I was safe—at least for now.

Chapter 40

Cliffside

The glow from the scattered candles made the beige limestone patio feel warm and inviting. The front section was for dining and entertaining, but the back was a sloping garden leading to a lounging area with views over Paris. I cringed when I noticed the small table set up near the edge. I had wandered out to this cliffside view several times but had never walked this close. As I ran my hand along the iron fence's railing, I gave it a little tug to test its sturdiness. That's when I noticed the horizontal cables below, spaced very close together. I couldn't imagine how his wife could have fallen from here, but I was definitely not going to bring that up in conversation tonight.

Settling into a wrought iron chair with overstuffed cushions, I allowed myself to relax and enjoy the view that sat in front of me. The lights of Paris are a real thing; the city seems to glow at night. I was so lost in my Parisian scene that I didn't notice the young man in front of me holding the bottle of Prosecco. It startled me when he popped the cork. My arms flew up for protection as I jumped back in my chair. Luke laughed, but the wine opener was very upset. He quickly came to my side, showing me the bottle of wine while rattling off what I assume to be his apologies in French.

"You've done nothing wrong," I said, trying to reassure him. Finally, I grabbed the glass from the table, smiled gently at him, and asked, "May I have a glass?" He smiled and began to pour. I noticed my hands were shaking as the liquid began to accumulate in the glass. Maybe I wasn't as relaxed as I thought.

The staff brought a large tray of desserts and set them on our table. After choosing one, I shamelessly took a second one. Then, as I began to take a long sip from my glass, Luke blurted out, "I'd like to buy your painting." The statement didn't surprise me, but the way he said it did. It was condescending, as if I should feel lucky that he liked my work.

Swallowing hard, I answered, "I don't have a painting for sale. I'm not sure what you're referring to."

"I'm willing to pay you whatever you want for it. Name your price," he continued.

I didn't know what to say. Where was this coming from? "Luke, I don't know what you're talking about. I don't have a painting worth purchasing."

He laughed, a cold, bitter laugh. Turning to his staff, he ordered, "Leave us." He watched as they dispersed. One of them turned back to me and raised her eyebrows as if questioning my safety. I nodded curtly, and she joined the rest of the staff. He turned to me and smiled, then grabbed the Prosecco and filled my glass almost to the rim. "Don't play coy. You know you painted a masterpiece. And I want it."

I wondered if he had said the same thing to his wife. And I wondered if her "no" sealed her doom. My eyes went straight to the railing, then back to him. He wasn't a big man. I was pretty sure I could get away from him if he came after me. That was, unless he had a weapon. That's when I saw movement in the nearby bushes. A man with some sort of case. It was so dark that I couldn't make it out well, but I watched as he placed it on the ground and pulled something out. I was in trouble; he had help. Turning my attention to him, I forced myself to speak calmly. "Luke, I'm sure we can work this out. Call your man up and let's try to talk this through." My eyes bounced from Luke to the man in the darkness.

Luke seemed confused and followed my gaze just as the man began to approach. Then, ever so slowly, the shaded man lifted something into his arms. I was confused by its size; it certainly wasn't a gun. The bellows from an accordion filled the air as the sounds of Paris flowed around me. My exhale came out in the sound of a whew as a small laugh of relief washed over me. That's when it hit him. "You were scared? Of me? Good gosh. Why?"

I stammered for a second before admitting, "Well, if I'm being completely honest, this hasn't been a very lucky spot for you, back here on the side of this cliff."

He roared with laughter. "So, you thought I lured you out here to kill you?"

"Well, when you put it that way, it sounds crazy," I said with a shaky voice before realizing I was biting the inside of my lip. I made myself quit.

He stood, thanked the musician, and dismissed him. When he sat back down, he scooted his chair closer to mine. Leaning in, he said, "Janine, I'm in trouble and I need to buy your beautiful painting. The one of the streets of Montmartre. My whole career depends on it."

I nodded slowly, took a bite of my dessert, and another long sip of the sweet Prosecco. "I hear you, and I'm not saying no, but I need you to be completely honest with me."

"Okay. I can do that."

"I have many questions."

"And I'm ready to answer them," he replied, before taking a sip from his glass.

I jumped straight in. "You didn't paint any of your masterpieces, did you?"

He began to choke on his wine. When I stood to help, he waved me off, holding up a finger to give him a minute. A few coughs later, he answered. "How did you figure that out in such a short amount of time? No one else has."

"I was privy to information that others weren't. You let me into your life—your home, your studio, and your flat in Avignon. I found your room of paintings there, and they were good, but they looked nothing like the paintings you now claim to be your own. I knew right away. Probably because I'm an artist, too."

"Why didn't you say anything earlier?" he asked.

"I almost did, but then I realized if you wanted me to know, you would have told me."

Luke leaned his elbows onto the table, ready to talk. "It all began as a mistake. About a year after Eliana passed away, I finally got up the courage to go into her studio. That's when I found her paintings. They were beautiful and I wasn't sure what to do with them, so I asked Renae. She questioned if anyone else knew about them before asking to take one to study further, and the next thing I knew, she had it displayed in the window of my gallery with my name as the artist."

"I don't understand. The artist is listed as L Depris, not E Depris. How did she change it so quickly?"

"My nickname for Eliana was L. She signed every note she left for me as L. I was shocked when I saw she signed her paintings that way, too," he answered, his voice cracking at the end of his sentence.

"Renae played you," I blurted out. "I knew I didn't trust her. So, why didn't you sue her?"

Luke went very quiet. I could tell he was upset, but I didn't interrupt his train of thought.

"I threatened to, and almost did, but Renae convinced me to be silent. She said the world deserved to see Eliana's great art, which I completely agreed with. Then, when the money started rolling in, I was able to do so many good things for the community. And before long, the lie became a reality. That is, until I released the fourth painting."

I felt sorry for him in a way. I'm not sure why, but I did. "And now, Renae demands more?" I asked.

"Yes. She found a small painting in an antique shop that she claimed could pass as one of Eliana's, but it hadn't been kept well and was darkened by age. So, she tracked the artist down and found him in the States—your grandfather. But as soon as she saw he had passed away, she found you. Sweet, talented, beautiful you."

I stared out over Paris while processing his story. I hadn't realized I was rubbing my Miraculous Medal that had fallen free from my dress until I turned back to Luke. He appeared to be holding his breath as he stared at the medal. I'd seen this look of total fear on his face before. The first time was when he was telling me that he was being haunted by his late wife, and the second time when he saw my medal in Avignon and fled. I knew I needed to tread lightly, but a small part of me was enjoying it. I sat still for a second before holding the medal up to him, saying, "I know Eliana wore one too; am I right?"

He only nodded.

"I traveled to Paris and spoke with Sister Louise at the Daughters of Charity. She explained the family story to me. She told me about when the Miraculous Medal began and its high demand. She said there was a family of goldsmiths in Montmartre who asked to speak to Saint Catherine of Labouré herself. It is said that she was so impressed by the family's humbleness that she asked them to craft a special medal to be passed down to recognize the artists in their family. It was silver and had a ruby red rim. She told me that she thought the last one had been buried with its owner a few years ago."

"Eliana," he whispered.

"Yes, Eliana. But this one..." I said, holding mine up, "was my grandfather's, who obviously was an artist from the family, too. And he gave it to me."

Luke shook his head. "So, Renae must know this story, too."

"She must have, to send someone across the Atlantic Ocean in search of another artist."

"You're right. She's been playing me all along, and now she's after you."

"Well, I'm not much to go after at present, but yes, it appears that way."

"Let me think on this for a bit, okay?" He didn't wait for an answer before standing from the table, suddenly in a hurry to get somewhere. "I'll walk you back to the studio."

He left me in the doorway and hurried off down the path, barely saying goodbye. I fiddled for my key, laughing that I had listened to Jorge's warning to lock my door. Only, as soon as I walked in, I realized that someone had been there. And that person had taken two of my paintings.

Chapter 41

Self Portrait

I stared up at the ceiling, still reeling over the fact that someone had stolen from me. I knew it was Renae, but how could I prove it? I had called Luke, but he was nowhere to be found. Instead, Jorge showed up almost immediately, almost as if he had been lingering outside in the courtyard.

"Please don't call the authorities. I'm sure we can work this out," he had said.

"How much do you know?" I had asked Jorge.

He cleared his throat and said, "Everything."

I blew out a sigh of relief. "So, we're pretty sure who took them?" I asked.

"Them?"

"Yes, two paintings were taken."

He seemed perplexed, but reassured me, "I'll get to the bottom of this."

Honestly, it didn't upset me very much. The possibility of someone stealing something I had painted was almost amusing. I had begged people to buy my work in New York without ever getting very far. When I was sitting with Luke at dessert last night, I decided to give him the painting. Still, I'd love to put Renae in her place.

After a restless night of sleep, the sound of the coffee machine beeping its completion pulled me out of bed. I poured a cup, and before taking a sip, I decided to walk out by the fountain to enjoy my first cup. It was still early, so I didn't mind being in my cotton short pajamas. No one would be up yet. I was only halfway out the door when I realized how cool it had become. The rain had fallen softly during the night, but I had no idea how much it had affected the temperature outside.

I settled into a chair that was covered by an open umbrella. My toes tingled from the cold, but I was determined to enjoy my cup of coffee outside. Pulling the cup close to my nose, I enjoyed the earthy aroma mixed with the warm steam before taking the first sip. "Mmm," I groaned with delight before taking the second.

While enjoying my coffee, I let my eyes run the length of my cottage. It was such a cute addition to the beautiful home. But for the first time since I arrived, I noticed the imbalance of the windows. I usually picked up on such things, so it surprised me how well it had been covered by plants and tall bushes. The back wall appeared to be about fifteen to twenty feet from the last window. Yet, from the inside, the back wall began only a couple of feet from the window. I stared for the longest time, trying to make sense of it. Curiosity got the best of me after taking my last sip of coffee, so I got up and walked to the outer wall. I climbed through a flower bed and behind bushes, and sure enough, the builder had left open space in the back of the cottage.

That's odd, I thought. *The cottage could sure use that extra space. Why wouldn't they have finished it in?* My mind spun the thought until I finally decided it wasn't my business. Wet and cold, I walked back to the studio. As soon as I shut the door, I ran and jumped back into the bed, searching for warmth. But my mind wouldn't let go of the need for an explanation.

"All right, I'll look around a bit," I said to no one. Knocking on that back wall, I noticed the hollow sound. I went to the wall in front and knocked again. It made a thud. They definitely sounded different. Going back to the fake wall, I followed it, knocking my way around until it ended at the bathroom.

Wait, I remember getting ready for my fake date with Luke and the cold breeze coming through the side wall that held three hooks. I walked quickly to the closet and held my hand up to that space. I could still feel it. I climbed inside the small closet and pushed that small wall, but it didn't budge. I was about to leave when a thought came to my mind, almost as if someone had whispered it. *Pull.* So I did, and it opened.

A chill ran up my spine as I looked inside a large room. It was narrow but long and full of easels and shelves. I stood motionless. I was intruding. Still, I had come this far for a reason. Once again, I spoke to the unseen presence. "Show me what you want me to see," I said aloud, then proceeded.

"Oh my word," I whispered when I noticed the artwork everywhere, both sketches and paintings. I wandered through them, pausing at each one. These were different from the ones I knew so well. These felt personal, almost maternal. Yet, I knew she and Luke had never been able to have children. These paintings may have been her way of working through the pain of infertility. She drew a boy over dend over. He was always just out of sight, a turned head, a large hat, playing in the distance or in aerial view.

I studied one of the boy playing, noticing the boy's backyard seemed to be cliffside, just like her own. He was surrounded by grass and a swing set. Still, it was so familiar. I had the oddest feeling of respect, but also pride. We were both tied to each other through a family tie. I knew that now.

The last painting was of a young girl holding an infant. The background made the painting seem very impressionistic, but the young woman seemed more modern—almost a contradiction. That's when my eyes were drawn to a small desk that sat on the same wall as the door I had just entered.

I walked to it slowly, both intrigued and scared by what I would find. There was a single file sitting on top, covered in dust from lack of use. I decided to look inside but resolved to not go snooping through any of the drawers in the desk. When I flipped open the file, I was shocked by the photo that lay on top. He was much younger, but I would recognize his face anywhere—Joseph.

The five-by-seven photo captured Joseph as a young teenager with longer hair and a bit of acne.

"What do you have to do with this?" I whispered while running my finger across the photo.

I can't intrude, I told myself and quietly shut the folder. But my fingers lingered above, questioning my decision. That's when I felt someone watching from behind. I spun quickly to the spot, only to find the painting of the young girl holding the baby. My eyes focused on the child's dark hair. *It couldn't be,* I muttered, drawing my eyes back to the young mother, but knowing the answer in my heart.

I turned back to the folder and quickly flipped it open. The page behind Joseph's photo was a birth certificate naming a fifteen-year-old Eliana Laroche as the mother while leaving a large blank as the father. *Poor girl, she was just a child herself.* I flipped through many other documents before finding an adoption certificate. It wasn't the names of the adoptive couple that caught my attention; it was their address. Joseph had given it to me. "You should stop by my house sometime and see my photographs. I live very close to where you're staying," he had informed me. I had no idea where he had lived before, but now I had to find out.

I sat for a moment, letting the pieces fall into place, before turning back to what I now knew was a self-portrait. I then walked slowly around the paintings, one by one, taking my time. *I can understand why she kept these hidden,* I thought. They were the paintings of a sad mother who watched her only child from afar. *This is how she processed her emotions, through her art.*

I walked back through the closet, setting it all back like I found it. This room would have to keep, at least for a bit longer.

Chapter 42

The Photographer

I had already rang the doorbell twice. My finger hovered over the button, contemplating pushing it a third time. I didn't want to be a nuisance. *The third time's a charm*, I thought as I pushed. This time, I heard footsteps.

Joseph swung the door open and seemed surprised to see me. "*Bonjour*, Jan. I didn't think you would come," he said, straightening his hair. I was in the middle of developing photos. I usually don't stop, but when the doorbell rang for the third time, I couldn't help but wonder if something was wrong. My father is getting up there in age and I worry about him constantly."

"*Bonjour*, Joseph. I had some time this morning and decided to take you up on your offer to view your photos. Is this a good time?"

"It's a perfect time. I was just finishing up the photos of the children stomping in the water around the fountain. Come in, I'll show them to you."

I smiled and followed him up the stairs and into his home studio. It took a minute for my eyes to adjust to the amber safelight. He waited patiently, then began showing me the photos. I was speechless. I had expected photos of kids jumping in puddles but was pleased by his use of light on the water. I flipped through them, enjoying each one more than the last. Once I came to the end, I said, "These are incredible?"

A smile spread across his face that made him appear much younger, almost like the teen picture of him in the cottage. "Do you really think so?" he asked. I nodded, so he continued. "This is a series of prints. I'm entitling them, "What Lies Beneath.""

I let the title linger in the air for a brief moment. Just like his series, his life was much more than what met the eye. Finally, I agreed, "That is a perfect title."

"Thank you, Jan. I needed a little courage before sharing them with Luke. I don't feel like he takes me seriously," he confided.

"No one can doubt your skill if they view your work," I answered. While I was deep in thought, my eyes landed on another photo. This one was of me playing in the water. I hardly recognized my carefree self.

Joseph caught me staring. "It's a great photo. It sums up 'summer' and you look so..., so French."

I laughed. "Isn't that ironic?" I snipped. "But thank you for capturing me so beautifully.

"You should have it," he said as he offered it to me.

"I couldn't," I answered.

"It belongs to you. It would be an honor. Share it with someone you love."

I thanked Joseph, but my heart gave a little tug as I realized I had no one to share it with. I thought of Eddie for the briefest second but pushed the idea back down.

"Now, can I offer you a coffee and pastry?" Joseph asked. My stomach growled at the question, so I agreed.

As we walked toward the kitchen, I looked out the back windows. "Could we take our coffee on the back porch?"

My question seemed to surprise him. Still, he agreed. So, we carried our snacks to the back of the house and chatted idly about art, the gallery, and Luke. As we finished, I asked him if we could walk to the back of the yard, where I could look out at the view of Paris. He agreed, so we walked and continued our talk.

We walked down the designated path that ran through the grass. The flowers and shrubbery were organized like an English garden. "It's beautiful back here; everything seems to have its place. It seems almost magical. What was it like growing up here?"

"Not as magical as you might think," he confided. "You hit the nail on the head. Everything has its place, except for me. I don't think my parents ever really figured out where I fell into that place. They had lived so many years without children that I think I threw them for a loop. And after my mother died, I was left alone, much of the time. Still am. My father is rarely in Montmartre. He is always traveling for work."

I listened, then began interjecting questions about his schooling and photography. Joseph's whole demeanor changed. He loved his work and his friends from the gallery. They had become like family to him, especially Sophie.

When we came closer to the edge, Joseph pointed out various buildings in Paris. His view was stunning, but nothing compared to Luke's view. I turned and scanned up the side of the cliff. Joseph watched and pointed out, "That's where you are staying." I was shocked at how well you could see Luke's cliffside viewing area.

"You can see anyone standing there perfectly," I remarked.

"Yes, I know," he mumbled. His voice sounded strange, so I turned to him. His eyes fell to the ground, then back to mine. "I saw her, Luke's wife." He paused before continuing. "She would stand right there at the overlook. I saw her quite often as a child. My parents sent me outside to play every day, and she would always wave at me, although I didn't know who she was. I'd wave back before going about my business. But that afternoon, she was leaning over the rail too far, and she fell. I watched her fall."

I leaned closer to him, "You saw her fall?"

"Yes," he whispered.

"That must have been awful for you," I said. Then I thought about Luke and the rumors that circulated about him pushing his wife. Before I knew what I was saying, I blurted out, "Do you happen to remember if you saw anyone with Eliana?"

"I remember hearing two women arguing, so I walked near the edge to see where it was coming from. That's when I saw Eliana."

"I hate asking this, but could she have been pushed?"

"That's what the police asked me, too. And the answer is, absolutely not. She saw me. Then, like always, she leaned over the rail to wave, but she lost her balance."

I felt tears stinging my eyes but didn't swat them away. "What did you do?" I asked.

He seemed very uncomfortable, but in a low voice answered, "I watched."

He must have seen my face change to horror, so he quickly tried to explain. "She didn't seem scared. She didn't yell or cry out; she just fell backwards. I felt guilty when I looked away, but I couldn't watch when she died." He paused briefly, then added, "Did you know they thought someone murdered her?"

I only shook my head.

"I overheard the news program my parents were watching one night, reporting that Eliana Depris had fallen off the cliff and they were ruling it as a homicide. I tried talking to my dad, but he ordered me not to get involved. However, I was so upset that I confided in my teacher the next day at school, and once she was involved, the whole story came out. My dad wouldn't speak to me for weeks."

His eyes turned to me, so I smiled once again.

"I'm sorry, Joseph."

"No big deal. It was a long time ago."

As we walked back down the path to Joseph's childhood home, I noticed my surroundings from a different viewpoint. I could picture the scene. A young mother holding an infant son. The grass. The path. The house. And a long walkway covered with a blooming wisteria vine. Eliana had been here. She kept an eye on her son. She made sure Joseph was happy. If only she had been happy, too.

Chapter 43

The Red Door

This really doesn't concern me, I kept telling myself. And, in all actuality, it didn't. But the damnable trickle-down effect pulled many people from under the umbrella. The moment I found out about the family legacy of the Miraculous Medal, I became involved. The deal was sealed when Luke offered to purchase one of my paintings. *How should I proceed?* In all honesty, all I wanted to do at this point was plan my trip home. But I knew in my heart that I must bring some closure to this mess.

I was deep in thought as I walked up the driveway and was surprised to see Jorge sitting in the courtyard with my cottage door standing open.

"Hey Jorge, what's going on?"

"Is the studio haunted?" he blurted out.

I was shocked by his question but answered directly. "Yes, it is. And I believe I know who it is haunted by."

"Eliana!" he exclaimed. I nodded my head in agreement. "I came by to tell you about your painting at the gallery, and your door was open. I called out for you and walked inside. I felt like a breeze was pushing me towards the bathroom, and I worried something had happened to you, so I followed. You wouldn't believe what I found."

"A room full of Eliana's paintings," I answered.

He was stunned. "Yes," he mumbled. "You've seen everything in there?" Again, I nodded.

"The photographer?"

"Yes, everything."

"We need to tell Luke. He should tell us how to proceed," Jorge said.

I thought for a brief second. *Yes, this is Luke's story. Jorge is right.* Luke needed to tell us how to proceed. "I agree, Jorge. I'll tell him." As he stood to leave, I asked, "What did you want to tell me about my painting at the gallery?"

"I'm sorry. Whoever stole your painting has hung it in the gallery with Luke's name on it," he blurted out before stumbling off. He was shaken up. So much so, I contemplated going after him. But I had bigger fish to fry, and that fish was named Renae.

I practiced what I was going to say to her all the way to her house. The staff had given me her address but no directions. It took me much longer than expected to find my way. As I stood in front of the red door, I thought, *How suiting that her front door is red. The color invokes anger.* I lifted my hand to knock when the door flung open. Luke was making a rapid exit.

As soon as he saw me, he began making apologies. "I'm so sorry, Jan. I should have stopped her sooner. Now she is doing to you what she did to me."

I saw movement behind Luke. "Christine? What are you doing here?" I felt the tension bouncing between her and Luke. "What's going on?" I asked, looking from one to the other.

"I think you need to come inside and sit down," Luke

suggested, then, turning to Christine, he said, "Will you please put on the kettle?"

I followed Christine to a small kitchen in the back of the flat and sat in a chair at a small bistro table. Before my rump even hit the cushion, there was a hammering knock on the door.

"Good gosh, what now?" Luke asked and made his way back to the door.

In walked poor Jorge, in shock over his spectral encounter, while still coming to speak his mind to Renae. He glanced around the room and his eyes settled on me. Worry was written across his face, almost in a paternal way. "Are you okay?" he said softly. As soon as I nodded, he turned his attention to Luke.

"As each of you know, we are gathered in Renae's home. What you may not know, is that it's Christine's home, too," Luke announced. All eyes turned to Christine, who was staring a hole in the floor. Luke continued. "Much to my surprise, Renae is Christine's mother. She encouraged her daughter to apply for a job with me to keep an eye out on all of us. What Renae didn't seem to understand is that Christine has a kind heart."

Christine turned to Luke and began to cry. "I'm so sorry," she said softly to the group.

"Why don't you tell them?" Luke said to Christine.

"All right. I know my mum is not the best person in the world, but still—she's my mum. She helped me get the job, and I really, really love my job. Well, minus the sneaky part of keeping her informed." She cleared her throat and proceeded. "My mum was desperate to release a new painting by Luke. With each release, she received 25% of the profits. Luke makes a lot of money, so as long as he's putting out new art, she gets paid. She knew they had used Eliana's last painting, so she followed the family line and found Jan. She forced Luke to push Jan into giving him her painting. She just didn't expect Jan's high moral character."

Turning to me, Christine added, "It's refreshing. I admire you."

Christine continued. "My mum planned to steal Jan's painting and she wasn't going to wait any longer. So, I stole it before she could."

Jorge interrupted. "You stole the painting?"

"Yes," she answered while walking into the hallway and coming back with the rolled canvas. She handed it to me. "I'm very sorry, Jan. I made a knee-jerk decision and thought I had solved the problem. I had no idea she'd just grab one of your other ones."

"You mean my painting of the lavender fields is hanging in Gallery Laroche?" I asked.

Christine only nodded.

I laughed, remembering how love-struck I was when I painted it. It was almost a blur. Christine's brow furrowed at the sound of my laughing. Somehow, I felt the need to reassure her. "Truly, I'm not upset. Everything will work out exactly as it's supposed to." I stood to leave, but no one else moved.

"Luke, can I have a word as soon as you get back to the house? I'm going to the studio now and will be there until we speak."

"Yes, I need to settle a couple of things, but I'll be along shortly," he answered.

I glanced back at Luke before I left. He was sitting between the person who handled his everyday personal life and the person who handled his everyday business life. Other people might find that impressive, but I'm not one of them. I stood a little taller, grateful that I was totally in control of myself. Christine had even said she admired me. I must be doing a damn good job of handling my life!

Chapter 44

Secrets

A secret will only remain a secret if it's never shared. Once it's known, it becomes the decision of its holder whether to keep or disclose. The burden then lies on their back.

After a short time, I was ready to share my discoveries about the back room in the studio. It was up to Luke to decide what to do. I could picture Joseph's face as we stood in his backyard. I wished I could intervene and tell Joseph everything myself, but I now understood that it's not my secret to tell. Luke would decide how to proceed; I hoped he would do the right thing—this time.

I made sure that everything was in order when I arrived back at my cottage. The secret doorway was closed, and the hooks were all in place. I wanted Luke to see it just as I had.

Before I even realized what I was doing, I pulled my suitcase from under my bed and began to pack. The feeling had caught me by surprise. So subtle yet pressing. I probably wouldn't have noticed what it was had I not felt it before when I was living in New York. I was homesick.

I guess it's time to head back to Savannah, I mumbled as a tingle of excitement hit my stomach and made me smile.

———

THE KNOCK CAME LATER THAT AFTERNOON. I WAS IN THE process of taking my canvases off their frames and rolling them one by one. I quickly put everything aside and opened the door.

Luke immediately saw my suitcase and scanned the room, seeing the many piles I was planning to put inside. "You're leaving?" he asked. The sound of hurt weighed heavily in the air. I said nothing. "How could you leave me now, when all of this is about to explode?"

I wasn't going to be guilted into anything, and I wasn't going to let him distract me from what still needs to be done. "Luke, I need to tell you something."

He pointed to my luggage. "Yes, I see. I know you're leaving."

"No. It's not that. Now, try and put everything else from today behind you." He huffed loudly, so I reiterated, "I'm serious. What I'm about to show you will change your life forever." This got his attention. He nodded slowly, but didn't say a word, so I began. "The other day, I was sitting in the courtyard beside the fountain, having a cup of coffee, when I noticed something strange. The outside walls of the studio don't line up with the inner walls. I went over it several times in my mind, comparing the outside and inside areas, but the rooms didn't match the outside footprint."

He interrupted. "Why are you telling me this? Especially right now. We have much bigger problems."

"Bear with me," I said softly. He nodded again. "A few weeks ago, I noticed a strange air draft from the bathroom closet, so I began to snoop around. I found something you need to see."

A crinkle formed on his brow. Now, he was interested. "Lead the way," he replied.

We walked into the restroom, and I opened the closet. I then moved the shelves to the open position and went through. When I turned to tell him to follow, he was standing at my side with the most horrified look on his face.

"How could she?" he whispered.

His initial blame surprised me. His pain was still raw. He couldn't let her rest in peace. He walked around to each painting until stopping at the mother and child one, which I now know to be Eliana and Joseph. "It's a lovely likeness of her." He then added, "I guess since she could never have children of her own, she created one in a painting."

I froze. He noticed. I didn't realize I had been holding my breath until I inhaled.

"What are you not telling me?" he asked.

I opened my mouth to speak but couldn't find the words. He didn't wait.

"What? You seem surprised. Remember, I told you that we weren't able to conceive," he said angrily, almost accusing me of being inattentive.

Finally, I came to my senses and walked over to the desk. "There's more," I said softly.

The intensity of his stare burned through me.

"I don't think I want to know any more. I've got to get out of here," he said frantically while walking toward the door.

"No," I pleaded loudly. My tone stopped him, making him turn to me. "You've been running long enough. You should know the truth. No, you need to know the truth. You can't start living again until you let her go. And she can't rest in peace until you do. I know it's hard, but you must see this through."

His lip quivered as he shook his head. Finally, he whispered, "Okay," with a sorrowful puff of air, and walked to my side.

The lump in my throat was so tight that I couldn't speak. But Joseph deserved to know, so I swallowed hard. "I found these on her desk."

He sat in the desk chair, something I never felt I had the right to do, and began to flip through the papers. He dabbed his eyes several times over the course of the next few minutes, grunting and groaning while shaking his head in disbelief, then he closed the folder. Leaning onto the desk, he rested his head in his hands. I stood still, completely quiet.

"Did you read all of these?" he said slowly, the hurt dripping from each syllable.

"Yes. I'm sorry."

"Please, don't apologize," he said, turning to look me in the eyes. His voice cracked as he muttered, "This changes everything, doesn't it?"

I nodded my head while wiping the tears from my cheeks, but said nothing.

"Does Joseph know?"

Clearing my throat, I answered, "No. It wasn't my place to tell him."

"Thank you, Jan. I don't know how to ever repay you."

"I do. By making things right."

His lopsided smile gave me hope. He stood up, walked straight to me, and wrapped me in a hug before running out of Eliana's lost studio room. I felt the painting's presence, as if she were waiting for me. "I'm not sure what will happen next, but he knows. It's now up to him." I looked deeply into her painted eyes, letting the words I had just spoken sink in. Everything was now up to Luke. I was now free to go. "Goodbye, Eliana," I said with a smile. I was grateful I got to know the painter she was. The woman she was. The mother she was. It was time for me to go home. I offered a prayer for this incredible woman, then added one last thing. "May you rest in peace."

I left the room the same way I had found it. I shut the door inside the bathroom, rearranged the shelving, threw the rest of my clothes in my suitcase, and called for a ride to the airport.

Chapter 45

True Friends

As I sat in my cushy, first-class seat on the plane home from France, my thoughts tumbled in confusion. I wondered if the artistic gift I've had in France would transfer with me across the Atlantic Ocean. My mind quickly jumped to Eliana and then to Luke. I wasn't sure what he would decide, but I knew that sooner or later it would come down to this—the question of what lies beneath.

The news had spread across the world by the time my plane landed in Savannah. "Luke Depris is a Fake," was the headline I read as I walked quickly past the paper stand inside the airport. The television blaring outside of one of the gates showed dozens of reporters hovering outside of his Montmartre home, just waiting to get a story. The couple waiting for their luggage claimed they always thought he was too good to be true, but I didn't take their bait. I knew the whole story. My friends weren't the least bit affected by the news when they came barreling into baggage claim.

"Hey, sugar-pie," Kathleen called from the door. "We're here."

I felt a catch in my throat when I turned to see them all huddled together. Leaving the spinning carousel of luggage, I ran into a big group hug. Tears fell from my eyes; I had missed them so much. They each began reassuring me. "It's okay. We're all here for you," they said. But leave it to Latrice to change direction quickly. I felt her eyes on me as she backed away. Looking me up and down, she asked bluntly, "What the hell happened to you?"

I glanced down where her eyes had just surveyed me. "What do you mean?"

This time, she used her finger as she spoke, pointing out the things that confused her. "You're wearing white pants rolled into Capri's and a pale blue shirt. There's nothing bright and funky on your whole person. What did Paris do to my colorful friend?"

I thought for a second. "I know I'm colorful. I don't need to scream it with what I wear for everyone else to see it, too." Then, I reached down past the waistline of my pants and pulled out the top of my hot pink bikini briefs. "But just 'cause you don't see it don't mean it's not there."

The tribe hooted with laughter as we all wrapped each other into one big hug.

"We're all back together again," Agnes called out.

We all began talking at once and almost missed my bag coming around again. Thankfully, Maggie was standing closest. She reached up and plucked it off the belt, like it didn't weigh a ton.

"Dang, Maggie. You been lifting weights?" Stephanie asked.

"I'm in the middle of kayak season; I have to stay strong," she answered.

Agnes squeezed Maggie's bicep. "Mrs. Lardin would be so

proud of you. Remember when she had us bench pressing in P.E.?"

"No, but I remember learning how to square dance," Kathleen commented. "Now, swing your partner round and round, and..."

"Do-si-do!" they all cried out.

My heart was full as I looked around the group. During the last ten minutes, I had forgotten all about Luke's lies, his sorrow, and even the ghost of his dead wife. They helped me into their car and then drove me back to my apartment.

"We'll help you get your bags inside," Latrice said. The group snickered. I looked around to see why, but everyone was straight-faced, so I led the way inside.

"I got your mail like you asked," Aggie remarked as soon as we walked in the door.

"Anything good?" I teased, shocked when she answered, "Yes!"

She handed me an envelope that had been opened. "You told me if anything came from the college to open it, so I did."

All of my friends began to giggle.

"What? Tell me!" I demanded.

"I think we should show you instead," Agnes answered. She pulled me to the couch and turned on the television. "We're having a watch party. Since we weren't able to go to your graduation, we wanted to watch it with you.

My stomach clenched with dread. I had forgotten all about my fall down the stairs after I had received my diploma. But there it was, for the whole world to see, and it had been a doozie. I missed my step and then slid down five steps on my backside. When I stood up, I pulled down my dress that had gathered around my waist and repositioned my underwear that had been propelled into the great beyond.

"It was so dark; I thought no one had seen anything," I cried out despairingly to the group.

"Videos don't lie," Agnes retorted. "The recorder's light caught it all—up close and personal."

I buried my face in a throw pillow as they backed up the video and showed it again. Then again. I eventually peeked out to see their smiling faces. They loved me, through good times and bad. I began to laugh along with my friends, grateful to be home.

From then on, my graduation was referred to as "the great fall." And in some ways, it had been.

―――

AFTER I WALKED MY FRIENDS TO THEIR CARS, I NOTICED the kitchen light was on in my mom and dad's house. I wasn't surprised. My mom always practiced her new recipes late at night. She said that was the only time that my dad wouldn't try to pick at what she was cooking.

I swallowed down the lump in my throat, the kind that develops when you need to talk to someone who loves you unconditionally. I ran across the yard and entered through the kitchen door in a whirlwind. My mom turned, startled by my entrance, but as soon as she saw me, her face lit up.

I began to weep as I ran into her arms. She didn't ask any questions or even say a word; she just rubbed my back and hugged me until I was ready to talk. I had been through so much in France, and now all I wanted was to spill my guts to my mom.

I told her everything, from Luke asking me to go to Paris to finding the hidden room of art. She had many questions as we talked through the night. She cried openly as we retraced her father's young life, and when I was finished, she asked many questions about her relatives, Robèrt and Anne, and my grandfather's medal.

"I know a little more about this story," she admitted when I had finally reached the end. Clearing her throat, she began, "My dad and I had many long talks in the last few years of his life. He told me about leaving France, then he told me about Anne. Both he and his cousin, who was also his best friend, Robèrt, were in love with her. She chose Robèrt. He said that leaving France was the best decision of his life because he met my mom, who turned out to be the love of his life, and he found his home in the welcoming community of Savannah."

My mom began to cry when she got to the end, so I reached out and squeezed her hand.

"I'm so proud of you, Jan. You're fearless."

Still holding her hand, I basked in my mom's approval before answering, "I know where I got it from."

"Your grandfather," she stated.

"No. I got it from you." I motioned to her shelves of cookbooks and watched her eyes follow. "You've traveled to several countries searching for amazing food to share with the world. People love your recipes, but more than that, they love the stories behind them. When I was a little girl, Grandfather told me that your cooking and cookbooks were your form of art."

"He did?" she asked.

I squeezed her hand once again. "Yes, he did."

This time, it was my mom who was basking in her father's approval. She sat up straight and said, "You know, I've been thinking about going to France next year and doing a cookbook about Montmartre. But this time, I would need an assistant who could introduce me to the locals. Could you recommend anyone?"

I smiled as thoughts of Anne, Robèrt, Joseph, and the team of artists at the studio ran through my mind. Pointing to myself, I said, "I know just the girl."

She pulled me into a giant hug and whispered in my ear, "I do, too."

Chapter 46

The Aftermath

Luke peeked through his office shutters only to find the crowd of reporters was still gathered at the end of his driveway. He wondered how long they would barricade his house. He could barely believe all that had happened over the past twenty-four hours and how quickly news had spread. He had called an emergency press conference only that morning. It was strange to him how he'd kept a secret for so many years, but now it was an emergency to tell the truth. Still, when you're ready, you're ready. He had to pull the Band-Aid off quickly.

He began, "For the past ten years, I have lied to the world. I impersonated the most talented artist of this century. I put my faith in the wrong person, who advised me to take credit for something that was not mine. She told me it was all for the greater good of art, and I bought in. First, I told myself that my wife's art deserved to be seen by the world. Eliana Laroche Depris was an extraordinary artist. But I knew in my gut that I could have shown her work as her own and given her the credit she deserved. I was selfish, and many people were hurt in the process. Please forgive me. I will not answer any questions or comment further about what I've done. But please don't be jaded by my mistake. We have a beautiful art community here in Montmartre. Please continue to support one another and please know you'll always have my support. Thank you!"

It was done. Now, he would begin to pick up the pieces, although he wasn't quite sure what that looked like. Jan had proved to be a trusted friend and confidant. He knew he would miss her, in his own way. She had brought him truth and had encouraged him to do the same.

The press had a field day with his lies. They said horrible things about him, and there was no agent there to defend him. Renae had fled and the rich art collector she had sold Jan's painting to the night before had already filed a lawsuit against his studio. He was sure it would be the first of many, but he no longer cared. Strangely enough, he felt a light-heartedness he hadn't felt in many years.

Living a lie had been hard on him. He was ready to live a life of freedom. Sadly, the last twenty-four hours had shown him that it most likely couldn't be done in Montmartre. He needed an escape. A place where the people weren't personally invested in him. His thoughts jumped to the small seaside town he had found when he had visited Savannah that past May.

What was its name? He wondered. *Oh yeah, Tybee Island. Could I blend in there?*

He felt the smile begin to form as he remembered how relaxed he felt those days he visited. He longed for that feeling, now more than ever.

He had already figured out what he must do for Joseph and had written a large bonus check to Christine. She would be very comfortable until she found another job. Jorge was a different story. He was adamant about staying with Luke. Jorge told Luke he would move wherever he went. "I would prefer somewhere on a beach, but I'm not too picky," he had said.

Nodding his head at the prospect, Luke decided to do some research. Hopefully, he could find refuge on Tybee Island.

Chapter 47

Time Flies

The months that followed being home seemed to fly by. I hadn't spoken to Luke during that time, but I thought of him often. A lot had happened with him, but my only knowledge of his situation was brought to me through the media. They searched for him nonstop; everyone was scrambling to get an exclusive interview. Some had even conjured up stories of their own. The latest one was titled "Where's Luke?" The photo they used had taken a picture of Luke and had photoshopped the red-and-white striped hat of the famed "Waldo" character on top. They reported he had sold his house in Montmartre, his flat in Avignon, and that his studio had changed hands. My heart ached every time I thought about the beautiful Laroche Château being owned by an outsider. Knowing I had set that ball in motion made it even worse.

I tried calling Jorge to check in, but his number had been disconnected. I prayed everyone was all right. Well, not everyone. I hoped that Renae would get what she deserved. I still questioned if I should have pressed charges, but that ship had sailed and I had created many paintings since then. Still, I would love to have the memory of the lavender fields with Eddie. Or maybe it was better I didn't have that constant reminder. Now, I would never know.

Fall sped quickly, as did winter, and before I knew it, spring was afoot. That's when I received a letter from Luke. It was short, but to the point. He and Jorge had left France. He had told Joseph everything and left him his inheritance, the house in Montmartre and the studio filled with Eliana's paintings. He thanked me for giving him his life back and ended the letter with his hopes of one day seeing me again.

I read the letter three times. "He told him," I mumbled. "Joseph knows Eliana was his mother." Tears ran down my face as I thought about Joseph and his mother on the cliff. Somewhere during that time, my hand had come to rest on my Miraculous Medal.

It came to me, almost in a whisper, yet I recognized the voice. "He should have it. His mother would have given him the one she had. You no longer need it." I reached up and took my necklace from around my neck. Thoughts of my grandfather filled me, as if he were standing right next to me.

I grabbed a piece of paper and a pen and began to write, then dropped the letter and my most treasured possession inside.

———

THE ROUTINE I HAD BEGUN IN MONTMARTRE OF wandering and sketching had pilfered over into Savannah. I happily sketched and painted my way through every season, watching the city come alive in a way that I never knew possible while bringing local scenes to life. Every week, I'd complete a new piece and take it to Aggie's restaurant to display before marking it "For Sale." The arrangement seemed to be working perfectly, or at least I thought it was, until the day I was fired.

I was given the news at our regular lunch.

"Go ahead, Agnes. Tell her," Latrice said.

Agnes looked sheepishly toward me.

"Tell me what?" I asked.

"It's nothing, really," Agnes answered.

The sound of Latrice's nails clicking against the tabletop got everyone's attention. "Okay, then I've got this," Latrice announced. "The other day, I popped into Aggie's to sit at my favorite booth and get a cup of coffee and a cinnamon roll. But when I arrived, the place was packed. I'm talking wall-to-wall people. The funny thing was, no one was eating."

"It's not always like that." She turned to Jan to explain. "You had come by that morning and put prices on the pieces you were ready to sell."

Latrice continued. "When I asked Agnes what was going on, she said she didn't have time to talk because she was officiating a bid war between three clients. She actually called them clients."

All eyes flew to Agnes, who just shrugged. "It was kind of fun, even if it ran off customers."

I was shocked. "I had no idea, Agnes. I'm so sorry. I'll come get them first thing in the morning."

"It's not a big deal, Jan, but I think you have definitely outgrown my little restaurant," Agnes explained with a smile. "And that's a really good problem."

I reached over and squeezed Agnes' hand, saying, "Thank you, friend."

We were interrupted by Latrice. "See there, everybody. All

we got to do is communicate. Always communicate. It's the key to every strong group."

I took my napkin and threw it at her. "Okay, President Latrice, now simmer down. You wouldn't even be upset had it not affected eating your cinnamon roll at Aggie's."

Latrice looked upset at first but began to laugh when the others did the same.

"You don't mess with my cinnamon rolls. You should know that," she announced.

We all placed our orders as Maggie began to talk about her old friend Leo, who was a gondolier from Venice, Italy. He had come back to Tybee and was now helping her run her kayak business. She seemed to be flushed with excitement. Watching her made me think of Eddie. He would always be the one who got away.

The group's conversation shifted to the Rockin' in the School Year celebration coming to Forsyth Park again on the first weekend in August. Kathleen asked who was going, then added, "Jack told me to ask you guys over a couple of hours before for cocktails, and then we can walk to the park at eight."

"I heard the Chippewas were headliners again this year. Do you remember the lead singer last year? What was his name? Eddie something."

A cold chill ran through me. Eddie? Surely, not. But it seemed like I remembered him talking about playing in a group called the Chippewas. Finally, I asked, "Hey, I wasn't back from France last year when y'all went to the concert. What's this Eddie guy look like anyway?"

They seemed surprised by my question, but Stephanie answered. "He's sexy. Probably more your type than mine, but he sure can play the guitar."

I was lost in my thoughts and didn't hear Kathleen ask me a

question until all eyes turned to me. I shook myself to pay attention. "What did you ask?"

"You're the only one who hasn't answered. Do you want to come over before and walk to the park together?

"I think I'll just meet up with you guys there. I have something to do beforehand," I said, and was glad when they changed the subject.

Chapter 48

Eddie

I knew who the flowers were from before I ever opened the card. Lavender. They were the largest bundle of fresh lavender I'd ever seen in Savannah, with the most vibrant purple flowers. I picked them up from the stoop outside my apartment and carried them inside. Setting them down at the end of the kitchen counter, I pulled the card.

> You said you'd love to show me your Savannah. I'd like to take you up on that offer. Would you be free tomorrow morning?
>
> P.S. – In case you're wondering who sent these, it's Eddie, NOT tow-truck Vern.

Closing my eyes, I lifted the bouquet to my nose, breathing in the scent of a memory. Almost instantly, I was transported right back to that field in France, looking up through leafy stalks of Lavender into a blue sky. My head resting on Eddie's shoulder—I was happy.

My eyes flew open as the nervous tingle hit my stomach. I hadn't been ready for a relationship with Eddie while we were in France, but circumstances had now changed. I flipped over the card that had been sent with the flowers to find that Eddie had left his number on the back. Just like before, God was giving me yet another chance with Eddie, and I was going to take it.

———

Eddie and I spent the most incredible few days together. We picked up right where we left off. Over the course of the year, we had both come to a place where we knew what we wanted in life, which made our conversations more personal and intentional. The one thing that hadn't changed was his laugh. It could still cut me to the core, and he used it as a weapon against me, often to draw me in even further.

On Friday of that week, he asked me to a late dinner at 1790. Paris may be known to be the most romantic city in the world, but Savannah gives it a run for its money. We parked the car and walked along the tabby sidewalk, lit by gas-burning streetlights, until we came to the green awning of 1790 Restaurant. They sat us at a cozy table near the window where we could pull our chairs close to one another. The old Savannah Grey bricks seemed to change shades under the dimmed lights of the glass chandeliers.

"I wonder how many couples have sat in this exact spot, whispering their romantic secrets to one another?" I asked Eddie, just as the waitress approached the table.

"Hundreds of thousands, I would say," she answered. "Along with many people who may have been plotting murders and several people discussing military secrets." Eddie and I were shocked by her answer. He raised an eyebrow at me, and then we both smiled at our waitress.

"Hi, I'm Katie. Welcome. Are we celebrating anything tonight?"

"Found-again love," Eddie answered.

I felt the heat of a blush sting my cheeks. Katie seemed to notice it, too, and offered me a slight smile.

"Congratulations, you two. Take a look at the menu, and I'll be back with biscuits and to take your order."

I buried my nose in my menu like it was the most important thing I'd ever read. Eddie's exclamation had thrown me off guard, if I'm being honest. It was one thing to say in private and a whole different thing to announce to a stranger. I could feel his stare coming through the menu. I lowered it enough to verify and got caught.

"I made you uncomfortable."

"No, not really."

He gave me a side stare, questioning me with his eyes.

"Okay. Yes. I was a little surprised by your answer. But certainly not upset. You're right. Second chance on love."

The waitress returned at that time with the wine we ordered. He held up his glass in a toast. "In hopes that we sit in this booth many times in the future." Our glasses clinked and we both took long sips.

We enjoyed our biscuits with honey, then fried green tomato Caprese, followed by my Salmon Oscar and his rib shank, then finished with peach cobbler à la mode.

While sipping on our last glass of wine, I revisited the menu to read the page I hadn't finished. It told the story of the building and restaurant, then talked about each of its resident ghosts. When I finished, I scanned the room, imagining the ghosts enjoying this atmosphere. As I looked around, the only person staring at me was Eddie.

I smiled when our eyes met, holding his gaze while he seemed to be contemplating something. He began, "I came to

Savannah last year for a concert in Forsyth called Rockin' in the School Year. I agreed to play because I wanted to see you, but you were still in France. For whatever reason, I convinced myself that you had stayed with Luke. My pride got the best of me. I agreed to come back and play this year because I had to see for myself. I'm so happy I did. I love being with you, Jan. I look forward to getting to know you even better if you'll allow it."

"You were right when you said we were celebrating found-again love. I'm so happy we found our way back to each other," I whispered before leaning over and kissing him right there in the middle of the restaurant.

"Wow, I didn't see that coming," he muttered when I finally pulled back.

And I answered just as I did on the Pont du Gard bridge, "I like to keep you guessing."

We were interrupted by a yellow light flashing through the front window.

"Not again," Eddie yelled as he quickly threw cash on the table for the bill and grabbed my hand. The tow truck was just pulling off as we ran out the front door, but the driver stopped when he saw us waving and screaming. This time, we didn't even try to explain. We just asked for a ride back to the yard and climbed in the front seat.

Chapter 49

Back to School Bash

The Forsyth fountain seemed to glow from the colors of the afternoon sun. The late summer skies always seemed to show off more than other times of the year. While Eddie and his group were setting up for the Back to School Bash, I decided to walk to the fountain, like I had hundreds of times before. As soon as I hit the circular pavers, I began to slowly stroll around the fountain's base, watching the female robed figure that adorned the top. For some reason, I had never paid much attention to her. But today, I couldn't pull my eyes away.

She had a martyr's stance, which really didn't surprise me since she has been forever cast, holding a staff in one hand while her other hand balances its weight. But there was something in the tilt of her head, or her downcast eyes, that made me pause. I followed her stare into the fountain, and there it was—Savannah's light. My thoughts jumped to the face of my grandfather at his easel that morning I had found him in tears. "I found my light," he had said, bursting with pride. I had seen it again the morning I wandered, at first light, into his neighborhood in Montmartre and painted the scene all day in the café with Anne. I saw it at sundown in the lavender fields with Eddie, and I later captured it on canvas. I found the secret, the link between my two most favorite places in the world. Both Savannah and Paris carry the same golden hour.

I knew the term "golden hour" from art school but had never referred to it outside of a photography class. Now I could see how important it is in all art. I learned that trick in Paris when I would wake up before sunrise and hit the streets. There was always a touch of magic on the iconic buildings and walkways. Many mornings since I'd been back home, I painted by the warm light that accentuates Savannah's architectural details, and then again at sunset when the natural beauty of our waterways exploded in color.

It had been revealed to me through my French grandfather, and ironically enough, the lady in the fountain, who also came from France. I nodded at her before I continued my walk, but I knew I'd be back to see her again. Savannahians are like that. We never tire of the beauty of our city and will go back and visit the same monuments over and over again. We often find something new each time we do.

When I got back to the stage front, Eddie was finished with the setup. He watched as I climbed the stairs with an odd expression on his face. "What happened to you?" he asked.

I felt the grin on my face. "I don't know what you're referring to, sir," I answered slyly. This was my secret, and mine alone. A woman's not meant to share all of her thoughts, or accolades.

"Okay. I get it. I won't pry." He ran his fingers down my arm before taking my hand in his. Leaning in close, he whispered, "But I'll tell you one thing, that look on your face is sexy as hell."

I felt the flush on my face, which only made him let out a

naughty laugh, before one of the band members called his name. I watched him walk away before turning my attention to all of the people who had already arrived. I searched the crowd and found my friends in their usual spot. They had spread out tablecloths and chairs and were eating and having fun together. I hadn't told them where I would be, although I wasn't sure why. I was proud that Eddie wanted me with him, but our relationship was still so new. I wanted to keep it to myself for a little bit longer. As soon as the tribe knew, they would start asking questions, and the first thing they would point out is that long-distance relationships didn't work.

The concert was fun to watch, but I enjoyed watching Eddie even more. His love of music showed in everything he did. I could relate; I felt the same way about my art. One of my professors would always quote Mark Twain, saying, "Find a job you enjoy doing and you'll never have to work a day in your life." That motto applied to both of us.

While the four other bands each played their different styles of music, Eddie and I stood together on the sidelines, his arm draped loosely over my shoulder as we sang along. As soon as the last band left the stage, the stage crew ran out and arranged things for the headliner—The Chippewas. Eddie watched calmly as everyone did their jobs, then turned and gave me a kiss before running out on stage. It was as if someone pressed his "on" button. The calm man from the side began to jump around with the audience feeding his energy. I peeked around the corner to look for my friends and was surprised to see them dancing directly in front of the stage.

When the Chippewas finished their last song, they asked the other four bands to come back up on stage with them to play the final song, "Georgia on My Mind." I was surprised when Eddie pulled me onto the stage beside him, but not as surprised as the tribe was. They made their way over to where I was and stood under me, all swaying and singing. As the song ended, I looked down at them, held up the rock-on sign, and blew them a kiss. Eddie watched me and did the same. He blew them a kiss and held up the rock-on sign. They all screamed like groupies and couldn't stop laughing. He then whispered, "Is that your tribe that I'm meeting later?"

I beamed with pride, "It sure is. And I think you already made a great first impression."

Chapter 50

Mama's Teachings

It took a while for Eddie to help load up all the equipment afterwards. As I sat on the stone fence, I couldn't help but overhear a conversation between him and the drummer for the band. "Now that you'll be living in Savannah, we'll have plenty of time to practice new songs," the band member said.

"I can't wait to be in Savannah full time. The drive has been killing me," Eddie replied as they both disappeared into the back of a flatbed truck.

Eddie is moving to Savannah? Has he known that all along? My thoughts were interrupted when Eddie called out, "Hey, Jan. You ready?"

I hopped down from the fence. "We can walk from here," I suggested when he pulled his keys from his pocket.

He smiled and took my hand in his as we jotted across Whitaker Street. The streetlights popped on one by one as we passed underneath, while Eddie and I fell into a comfortable stroll.

"I love Savannah. Look how the lights from inside these

beautiful historic homes spill onto the brick pavement," he remarked.

"You should try living here. There's beauty everywhere I turn."

He stopped walking. "Actually, I have something I want to tell you. I didn't say anything before because I wasn't sure, but the college offered me a job. You remember that friend I told you about that I wrote jingles with?" I nodded. "Well, he is now head of the music department at the college and he offered me a job."

I couldn't hide my excitement. "Are you gonna take it?" I squeaked in a high-pitched voice I didn't recognize.

"That depends on you."

"Me?"

"Yes, you." He stepped in front of me, where he could look me in the eyes. Pushing a strand of hair away from my eyes, he said, "Surely you know I'm crazy about you, don't you?"

I wrapped my arms around his neck. "I'd really love it if you lived in Savannah," I admitted.

He leaned down and gently touched his lips to mine. Pulling away less than an inch, he whispered, "You'd really love it, or you'd really love me?"

I could feel his breath on my wet lips. "Both," I said as his mouth seemed to devour the words before they barely hit the air. Our kiss became stronger and deeper until I felt Eddie flinch.

"Hey, watch it," he cried out, jumping away from me.

I opened my eyes, dazed and confused, as Eddie turned to the older man.

"Why did you hit me, Pops?" Eddie asked the man with a cane.

"You are blocking the sidewalk. I waited for you to finish your business, but I could tell it was going to take a while, so I took matters into my own hands. Didn't your mama teach you not to neck in public?" the older man said.

"Didn't your mama teach you not to hit people with your cane?" Eddie answered.

The older man smiled. "Touche, young man. My apologies," he said, before turning to me. "Excuse my interruption, young lady," he said, as he walked around us.

"Have a nice evening," I called out to him.

He paused. "It most certainly won't be as nice as yours, but I had forty-five beautiful years with my soul mate. Those memories live on forever. Goodnight, Jan," he said before walking off.

I watched him walk away, trying to piece together who he was.

Eddie began to giggle. "Oh my gosh, your face. You look mortified. Did you know him?" Eddie asked with a giggle.

"I'm not sure. That's just how it is when you grow up in Savannah, people remember you and where you fit in the mix of this beautiful town."

Eddie smiled as he moved closer. Lacing his fingers with mine, he said, "I can't wait to fit in the mix as your boyfriend."

I stood on my tiptoes and kissed his cheek, "Okay then, boyfriend. But right now, we need to get to Kathleen's. Remember the promise you made me?"

"Time to meet the tribe?" he asked.

I nodded, but the trepidation in his voice had not gone unnoticed, so I added, "They are going to love you."

———

EDDIE GRABBED MY ARM WHEN I BEGAN WALKING DOWN the dark lane. I patted his hand. "This is the way to Kathleen's house," I explained.

"She lives on a creepy, dark lane with no lights? What is she, a witch?"

I thought for a moment before answering. "Not exactly, but she does see ghosts. Does that count?" He opened his mouth to talk, but I interrupted. "It's fine. This is the lane that runs behind the prettiest street in Savannah—Jones Street. We're just taking the shortcut. Trust me."

We walked in silence until we heard the sounds of laughter spilling down the lane. My pace quickened. "Come on, slow-poke. Those are my friends." The alleyway began to fill with light as we reached the back gate. I paused for a moment, watching them from behind the jasmine-covered fence. They all sat with their feet hanging into the new fountain Jack had just added to their beautiful garden.

Maggie saw us first and called out my name. "Jan! Get yourself in here!" Everyone else chimed in, welcoming us into the group.

Jack immediately jumped up, grabbed two beers, and approached us. He kissed me on the cheek, handed me a drink, and immediately shook Eddie's hand and introduced him to the rest of the group. Jack was always the perfect host and watched out for each one of us.

Kathleen turned to get up from the fountain, but I was already at her side. "I'm so happy you guys made it," she said, before adding, "He's a hottie, Jan."

"I know. And he's moving to Savannah," I said in a hushed voice. However, when you're part of a friend group, your hearing becomes ultrasonic when a secret is whispered, so I wasn't surprised when the others chimed in. I cut my eyes to Eddie, who was now in a deep conversation with Jack, before sharing the information a tad louder with my friends.

They all began asking me a million questions in their not-so-quiet whispers. Finally, Latrice put everything in place for us like she always does. "We need to know. What does his move to Savannah mean for us?"

I felt their eyes move above my head as Eddie walked up behind me. Placing his hand on my shoulder, he answered, "It means that you ladies are going to be seeing a lot more of me. And I can't wait to get to know you all."

Everyone happily welcomed him to Savannah, all calling out their greetings at one time. I reached up and held his hand that was still resting on my shoulder. I looked at my friends one by one. Each of their smiles warmed my heart. Jumping down in the fountain, I called out, "I hate to do this, you nosy little bitches, but you had this coming when you bombarded me with questions." I began to kick fountain water on the group, soaking each of them before they got in and did the same to me. Somewhere in the chaos, Eddie retreated back over beside Jack. When our eyes met, I blew him a kiss and threw up the rock-on sign. He smiled, nodded his head, and air kissed me back.

Chapter 51

The Gallery

The day had come for me to find a studio for my art. I had asked my friends at the art college if one place was better than the next, and the new studio on Bull Street got the best reviews. The gallery had actually reached out to me several times, asking if I'd consider displaying my art, but I'd been too busy creating to take the time to think about the business side of selling my art. However, it was time for me to find professionals to help me sell my work.

I searched through my old mail to find one of their letters for the contact name at the studio. Thoughts of France filled my head as soon as I pulled the letter from the envelope. Some days were like that. It was the beauty of Paris. A warm feeling. A glittering spark. I closed my eyes, imagining the imprint of people from the past who had walked the same paths before me. I always tried to capture the image so I could put it on paper, but somewhere in the recesses of my mind, I continued to search for its meaning.

It's no surprise that when I thought of France, I thought of Luke. I left while he was in turmoil, so there wasn't time for goodbyes. I tried several times to locate him, but true to his word, he had to go off the grid. I only prayed that he had finally found his peace.

Returning to the task at hand, I scanned the letter for the address and the owner's name. Something seemed so familiar, yet I couldn't put my finger on it. Maybe it would come to me when I got to the studio.

I hardly recognized the block on Bull Street when I turned the corner. Once run-down buildings had been transformed into nice shops and restaurants, with an art gallery sitting at the very end of the block. I sat in my car watching the people pass, ducking inside the stationery store or the French bakery and lingering outside the window of the gallery, admiring the paintings on display.

This is a good sign, I thought as I picked up the piece of paper with the owner's name from the passenger's seat and carried it toward the door. The building was beautiful with large picture windows and various plants growing in giant ceramic pots along the front. Once again, I was hit by the familiarity of the studio. *Maybe it's a chain*, I thought, as I pushed open the large wooden door and walked inside.

I was greeted immediately by a woman I recognized from the college who remembered me by name. "Hello, Jan, I'm so happy you came in. Can I help you with something?"

"Yes, I received several letters from the gallery's owner, Sir Pedekul, who asked me to come and speak to him about showing.

She walked to the counter and made a call, then asked me to follow her. We walked down a long hallway and out of the door of the gallery before entering a studio full of classrooms and exhibits. I'd never seen anything like it except for Gallery Laroche in Montmartre. It was even set up similarly. I was sad that I had been so out of the loop, painting alone, that I wasn't aware what had popped up right under my nose.

When we passed a class, I saw a man who looked almost identical to Jorge sitting in the front, teaching. I smiled at the memory of us throwing clay at each other. Finally, she stopped at the door on the end and knocked three times. A male's voice called out, "Come in." The receptionist opened the door and stepped back for me to enter, then closed it behind me. The curator had his back to me as he looked out the window, but I knew who he was. He slowly turned in his chair until I could look him in the eyes. I didn't wait for him to say a word before I ran around the desk and wrapped him in a hug.

He held me tightly before pulling back and kissing both my cheeks, in true French fashion.

"Janine, why did it take you so long to come?"

I laughed through my happy tears. Luke had disappeared from the world and was living happily right under my nose.

"I'm so sorry that I didn't figure it out sooner, Luke. I never got to tell you how proud I am of you for telling the world the truth. I'm so happy you found refuge here."

"Thank you, Jan, for leading me in the right direction," he said, squeezing my hands tightly in his.

I nodded with a smile as my eyes roamed his office. They landed on his nameplate sitting on his desk. "Sir Pedekul? Very witty that it's Luke Depris spelled backwards," I commented as I focused on his logo, etched on the window. "Gallery L," I whispered. You named your gallery after Eliana," I said, feeling the lump in my throat take shape when my voice cracked. He must have seen it, too.

"We'll have none of that," he said softly. "I need to show you something." He walked me out in the hall and down to the next room, which was filled with artwork. Opening a tall cabinet door, he pulled out a canvas and gave it to me.

"*Lavender Fields,*" I cried out. "How did you get it back?"

"The man who bought it from Renae handed it over voluntarily with one condition. If I ever hear from her again or find out where she's hiding, I'll turn that information straight over to him and his organization. And believe me when I say, he's not the type of person one would want to cross."

"So, it's safe to say she won't be able to hurt anybody ever again?" I asked.

"I'd say it's pretty safe. Yes. Now, let's get down to business. I want to show your art."

"Okay. Which painting?" I asked.

"All of them!"

Chapter 52

You Must Find Your Light

The growing mountain of mail sitting on the end of my kitchen counter had begun to sway. I had put off going through it because I had been so busy, but today was Saturday and for the first time in a long time, I had no plans. Pouring me a bowl of what I call my guilty pleasure, aka Peanut Butter Captain Crunch, I hopped up on the nearest barstool to pilfer through the pile. "Keep. Keep. Toss," I called out as I quickly tried to get through the task at hand. That's when I noticed Joseph's face on the front of my favorite art magazine.

"Up-and-Coming Photographer and Businessman, Joseph Laroche, Taking the World by Storm," was the title, spread across the black and white cover. I pushed my cereal bowl out of the way and spread the magazine out in front of me. He had changed his last name to his mother's. *Well done, Joseph.* The article told the story of a small boy who grew up loving photography after he was given a camera in elementary school. It told of him finding peers who encouraged him at a studio in France, although it didn't mention the name of that studio. Then it explained that he had recently discovered a lost member of his family who had left their inheritance to him. With that, he opened his own studio on the outskirts of Paris. The story ended with a quote from Joseph saying he was blessed to grow up with his father in a loving home in Montmartre and wanted to give back to his community, just as he had been given to.

I pulled the magazine closer, examining the photos scattered throughout the article. He looked handsome in the black and white images. His hair and his shirt seemed to be similar dark colors. I stopped when I got to the last photo. The expression on his face was priceless. It was one I had never seen in my short time of knowing him. He had an expression of contentment. I pulled the image closer when I noticed the shine of something hanging around his neck, already knowing what it was. My grandfather's Miraculous Medal hung naturally around Joseph's neck, almost as if it had been there all along.

I stared at it for the longest time and was surprised I didn't long for it back. Sister Louise had contacted him, just like I had asked her to do, and he had actually gone to her.

My heart beat a little faster as I thought back to that day when I sent her my medal. I explained in my letter to her that there was another blessed artist, sent her Joseph's name, and asked her to explain everything to him. He had been such a tortured young man, struggling with strong feelings of abandonment from his mother that no one could ever fix for him. The necklace gave him his place in the world. But more than that. If, like me, he developed a relationship with the Blessed Mother on the medal, it would give him the motherly love and protection he had always desired.

As soon as I finished reading the article, I had the strangest sensation, as if my grandfather was calling me. I dashed out the door without thinking, my feet leading me down the path I had now come to travel often. I anticipated the garden's iron gate to creak as I pushed it open and smiled in response. I was no longer the person I was when I found the marker. Montmartre had given me my place in the world—my piece in the bigger picture, where I was unique and special. I stand on the backs of many artists who had come before me, and now I must give legs to the ones to come.

My hands instinctively jumped to hold my necklace that was no longer there before I walked confidently to the marker he had left for me. Kneeling down, I placed my hand on the same spot I had come to know so well. I had seen both the light and darkness, good and evil. But it was in darkness that I found my true purpose, and it is in the light that followed that I could now create beautiful art for the world to enjoy.

THE END

Also by Leigh Ebberwein

The Blessing of the Celtic Curse

Kathleen Kenny embarks on a life-changing trip from Savannah to Ireland just before her wedding, where she confronts her dreams and discovers love and adventure that alter her future and the lives of two families forever.

The Savannah Gondolier

Maggie, a heartbroken kayak company owner on Tybee Island, and Leo, a troubled gondolier fleeing his past in Venice, must navigate their intertwined fates, confronting both the beauty of their surroundings and the emotional waters that threaten to pull them apart.

The Castle on Wassaw Sound

In a race against time, a determined local architect and a reluctant castle owner from Scotland must overcome their clashing personalities and trust each other to restore a historic Savannah castle before a land grant expires, uncovering secrets that could change their lives forever.

The Cottage on Mystic Lane

In a quest to unravel her late Aunt Lottie's enigmatic gifts and secrets, Agnes must confront a haunting past, navigate unexpected revelations about her adoption, and ultimately strive to forge her own destiny amid the mystical and emotional challenges that await her on Prince Edward Island.

STOP BY FOR A VISIT

If you love the beauty of Savannah and enjoy traveling the world through a novel, visit Leighebberwein.com. You'll find questions for your Book Club, live video scenes, up-to-date information on future books, and so much more!

facebook.com/Lebberwein

instagram.com/lebberwein

tiktok.com/@lebberwein